The Highlander's Choice

a Marriage Mart Mayhem novel

Other Books by Callie Hutton

The Elusive Wife

The Duke's Quandary

The Lady's Disgrace

The Baron's Betrayal

The Highlander's Choice

a Marriage Mart Mayhem novel

CALLIE HUTTON

Entangled Publishing, LLC
2614 South Timberline Road
Suite 109
Fort Collins, CO 80525
Visit our website at www.entangledpublishing.com.

Scandalous is an imprint of Entangled Publishing, LLC.

Edited by Erin Molta
Cover Design by Heidi Stryker
Cover Art by Period Images

ISBN 978-1-943336-60-9

Manufactured in the United States of America

First Edition July 2015

I dedicate this book to all of those involved in relationships of different cultures.
I have several in my family.

Chapter One

May, 1816
Dundas Castle, Scotland

Lady Sybil Lacey stepped out of the carriage that had held her prisoner for five long days on the journey from England to the wilds of Scotland. She stretched her tight, sore muscles and turned to her best friend, Lady Margaret Somerville, who alighted from the carriage next.

"It is very big," Margaret breathed, staring wide-eyed at the castle in front of them, her face a pale white. "How will I ever find my way around?"

Sybil patted her friend's hand. "Have no fear. You will doubtless know your way around before I leave to return home."

Margaret tugged Sybil closer to her side. "I wish you could stay forever."

In some ways this trip had seemed to *take* forever. For the first time in her life, Sybil and her twin, Sarah had been apart for longer than a few hours. As much as she was enjoying the journey and looking forward to her friend's wedding she'd felt as though part of her had been left behind in England.

Shaking herself from her ruminations, Sybil placed her hand firmly around her friend's waist, moving her forward and said, "Bridal nerves. That is all that is troubling you. You will be fine, and will no doubt be so enthralled with married life that you shan't even notice I'm gone."

Despite her encouraging words, Sybil thought her dear friend was cork-brained to consider marrying a Scotsman—and a Highlander, no less. The two friends, along with Sarah, had made their come-outs together. Since the Lacey girls were notorious among the *ton* for holding out for love matches, no one was surprised that despite very successful years, no man had measured up. The Lacey twins went year after year unspoken for. Much like their older sister, Abigail, who had only recently married.

On the other hand, Lord and Lady Somerville had told Margaret if she did not choose a man herself, they would do it for her. To Sybil's horror, but not necessarily it seemed, to Margaret's displeasure, her parents chose an occasional guest at their home, Laird Duncan McKinnon, a distant relative of Lady Somerville. And a Scotsman.

"This looks like a lovely home, Margaret," Lady Somerville said as she linked her arm in her daughter's. "I am sure you will be quite happy here at Dundas."

"Do you think so, mother? It is rather large." Margaret cast a doubtful glance at the woman.

Lord Somerville strode up alongside his wife and daughter. "No matter, my dear. I've no doubt you will do well."

The immense front door opened and Sybil started, prepared

to see huge beastly men charge out, shouting barbaric words and waving swords. As far as she was concerned, Scotsmen spent their time brawling, slaking their lust, and making whiskey. She had never met Margaret's betrothed and had no real expectation of a well-bred husband for her friend.

The two men who framed the doorway took up the entire space in the portal, despite its considerable size. Both men were well over six feet and as broad across the chest as a gorilla Sybil had once seen in a zoological book. She glanced at Margaret who had grown even paler.

"Which one is your betrothed?" Sybil whispered.

Margaret licked her lips and leaned closer. "Laird Duncan McKinnon is on the right. He is called The McKinnon."

Sybil studied the man as he and his partner both descended the steps and marched toward their group. As they grew closer, Sybil found herself stepping back, suddenly breathless as they blocked out the scant sun setting behind the castle. Good heavens, they grew them large in the Highlands!

"Lady Somerville." Duncan bowed over the woman's hand. "And my Lord." He nodded in Lord Somerville's direction. Then he turned to Margaret, taking her hand and raising it to his lips. "My dear. I am pleased to see you. I trust you had an uneventful journey?"

Margaret went from pale white to crimson as McKinnon bestowed a kiss on her hand.

"And is this your friend, Lady Sybil?" McKinnon turned to Sybil.

Still trying to recover her breath, Sybil closed her mouth, embarrassed to realize it hung open, and extended her hand to Margaret's betrothed. Then she glanced in the direction of McKinnon's companion. Any attempt to regain her breathing was lost as she took in the sight of mischievous eyes staring directly at her.

The man was a giant. There was simply no other word for it. His ginger colored hair touched his massive shoulders, surrounding a face much too handsome for a brawling Scot. Her glance roved down, over his trim waist, narrow hips and muscular thighs encased in tight breeches much like the ones English gentlemen wore. But no English gentlemen she'd ever seen had filled them out so.

The sound of The McKinnon clearing his throat drew her attention. Her heart sped up and heat flooded her face when she saw her friend's betrothed smirking in her direction. Oh good heavens, she'd been caught staring. Hopefully, she wasn't drooling, as well and she tamped down the urge to wipe her lips.

"Ladies and my lord, may I present my friend and neighbor, Liam, The MacBride." He paused, taking Sybil's hand. "Liam, may I make known to you my betrothed, Lady Margaret, her parents Lord and Lady Somerville, and Lady Margaret's friend, Lady Sybil."

The green-eyed giant took Sybil's hand and gave it a squeeze. His full lips tilted in a slight knowing smile. "My lady. 'Tis a pleasure."

Sybil drew herself up and made a quick curtsey, still trying to shake her reaction to the two large men. She pulled her hand back, feeling as though it burned where the laird's hand had touched hers. The grin and his mirthful eyes confirmed her opinion of Scots. What time they didn't spend drinking whiskey and brawling in the mud, they saved for lustful pursuits. She would need to stay far away from this one.

She breathed a sigh of relief when Duncan's friend turned

his attention to Margaret and Lady Somerville. Sybil took the opportunity to recover her dignity and study the castle that would be her friend's home. Despite the architecture indicating it as very old, it seemed well-maintained. A drawbridge lay across what, at one time, must have been a moat, but it was now dried up. It was a small structure, as castles go, but still imposing.

"My lady?" The MacBride extended his arm to Sybil, calling her attention back from the castle and to the group who now moved toward the entrance. She placed her hand on his rock-hard arm, noting that her diminutive size only brought the top of her head to his chin.

"Did you have a pleasant journey, lass?" Liam's deep voice slid over her like warm honey.

Disgusted at how her heartbeat sped up and her breathing once again hitched, she raised her chin. "There is nothing pleasant about being inside a carriage for five days." *Good heavens I sound like a shrew. Why am I snapping at the man for asking a polite question?*

She glanced sideways at her companion, taking in his tightened lips and shuttered eyes. Well, that was wonderful. She was out of the carriage merely minutes and already she'd managed to present herself as a bad-tempered harridan. Attempting a smile, she took a deep breath and said, "I apologize, sir. I fear the trip has left me more tired than I realized."

"I understand, I ken travel is a strain on a lady such as yerself."

There was one of those strange words that Scots insisted on using. Why didn't he just say he *knew* travel was a strain? How would Margaret adapt to this foreign land and peculiar way of life? And what did his comment, "a lady such as *yerself*" mean? Had she just been insulted?

Margaret and her betrothed chatted easily as they made their way across the drawbridge and into the castle. If her friend noticed anything odd about Duncan's language, or her surroundings, it didn't show. Perhaps it wouldn't be so difficult for Margaret to adapt.

The large door led them to a type of courtyard that surrounded the castle itself. She knew from her history that Highland castles at one time were "keeps" and the inside courtyard was where the clan worked, merchants brought their wares, and villagers gathered for safety when attacked by enemies.

"With no lady of the manor since my mum passed, I depend a great deal on my châtelaine, Mrs. Galbraith, to handle most things." He turned to Margaret. "I look forward to having ye take over those duties once we are married."

Margaret nodded briefly and threw a worried glance at her mother, who smiled encouragingly.

"Mrs. Galbraith has arranged for yer trunks to be brought up to yer rooms. She has also instructed that baths be prepared for the ladies." Duncan came to a halt and directed his comments to Lady Somerville. "We sup at six o'clock in the great hall."

Lady Somerville inclined her head and thanked their host. The three women proceeded up the winding staircase to the second floor, guided by a chatty, cheerful woman who waxed eloquent about all the preparations underway for the wedding in two weeks. Lord Somerville brought up the rear.

• • •

Liam MacBride shook his head as he watched the English party ascend the stairs, the women's hips swaying gracefully. "Ach, but you're in for a bad time, my friend." He slapped

Duncan on the back. "Princesses. All of them."

Especially the bonny lass who'd let him know the trip was not to her liking. No doubt she had complained the entire way. He would expect no less from the English.

"No. I think you hold a bit of prejudice against them." Duncan turned toward the library, Liam following. "'Tis something yer mum passed on. Not all English are the devils you think they are." He held up the decanter of whiskey, giving Liam a questioning glance.

Liam nodded and settled into a large chair in front of the fireplace. "Aye, I will enjoy watching yer betrothed lead you about by the nose."

"Nay. Not my Margaret. She is a sweet lass. The few times I've been in her company she was gentle and pleasing."

Liam took a sip of his whiskey and grinned. "Wait. Once the deed is done she will demand gowns and fripperies, and run yer servants into the ground. Englishwomen wish to sit about and gossip, drinking tea and eating biscuits. In no time, your lady wife will be plump and difficult."

His mum had the right of it. There wasn't much an Englishman was good for, and the women even less. Give him a sturdy Scottish lass, one who would warm his bed with lusty abandon. Not some scrawny Sassenach lying in bed like a stick, sighing her displeasure at her marital "duty."

"Lady Sybil is a bonny lass," Duncan said, glancing at Liam over the rim of his glass, reminding him of the shrew. "Mayhap she will keep ye from spending too much time pondering my fate."

Liam grunted. "A targe, that one." Truth be told, the lass was indeed a pretty little thing. Skin like a perfect white rose, with large eyes the color of fine whiskey. Her full lips were plump, made for kissing. Then the lass had opened her mouth and her beauty had shattered, crumbling before his very eyes like a day old biscuit. "No thank ye. Yer Sassenach is plenty."

"Ah, it appears I found the correct room." Lord Somerville entered the library, rubbing his hands together.

Duncan and Liam immediately stood. The older man gestured for them to sit and waved toward their glasses. "May I join you?"

"Yes, of course," Duncan said. He crossed the room and poured another glass of the brown liquid and handed it to his future father-in-law.

"To good health and a strong marriage between you and my daughter." Somerville saluted the other two men with his glass and downed the drink. "One thing I will say for you Scots. You sure know how to make a fine whiskey."

Somerville placed the empty glass on the small table next to his chair. "While the women do whatever it is they do to recover from a journey, I thought you and I might have a word?"

Liam stood. "I will leave you gentlemen to your discussion." He left the library and headed to the stables. A brisk ride along the river was just the thing to get his mind off the upcoming nuptials, and what a mistake his friend was about to make. Marrying an Englishwoman. He shook his head in disgust.

He tacked his horse, Cadeym, a massive black stallion with as much energy and spirit as its master. They raced from the stable, past the wooded area surrounding the castle, and onto the river. The wind whipping his hair in his face and the cool air in his lungs felt good.

Worries about his friend's marriage reminded him that the time had certainly come for him to choose his own wife. Although many of the lasses in his clan were bonny and had certainly let it be known they were interested, he hadn't found one he wanted to spend his life with. His parents' marriage had been a compatible one, but had lacked what he was looking for. He hated using the word "love" as that requirement, but that probably was what he'd noticed missing in his parents' relationship.

The gathering clouds dragged him from his musing. The approaching storm looked like it would be a good one. Slowing Cadeym down, he turned and reluctantly headed back toward Dundas.

About five miles from the stable he rounded a bend and a lad galloped toward him, head down, body low over the horse's mane. Did the fool not see the approaching storm? Liam shouted, but he whipped by, not paying him any mind. He glanced at the lad as he sped past, his jaw dropping when he realized the lad was not a lad at all, but the tiny English lass with the sharp tongue.

God's teeth, was the woman trying to kill herself? Had she no knowledge of how quickly storms blew up in the Highlands and how ferocious they could be? Here on the western side were some of the wettest and windiest places in all of Scotland.

He turned Cadeym once more and galloped after her just as fat drops of rain began to fall. He reached her just as she seemed to take in the weather for the first time. She glanced up, then turned to look at him as he came alongside her..

"And where do ye think yer going in this weather, lass?"

She slowed her horse, then pulled on the animal's reins until she came to a stop. "It is merely a bit of rain. I won't melt." The horse danced in place, shaking his head.

No wonder he'd taken her for a lad. She wore breeches,

snug around her bottom and legs. The white billowing shirt she wore tucked into her breeches was already wet, starting to outline her body beneath the cloth. Despite her small stature, she had a fine set of…

He snorted. A bit of rain, indeed. Just then the heavens opened to prove her a liar and dumped enough water on them to turn her shirt transparent.

"Oh." She glanced down at herself and wrapped her arms around her breasts. Water trickled down her nose, which she attempted to wipe off with her elbows, still keeping her chest covered. Her hair had been braided and wrapped around her head, but loose curls lay flat against her neck and forehead. She looked not much older than a bairn.

"I guess we better return to the stable." She blinked rapidly, trying to keep the water out of her eyes.

"Ach, ye think so, lass?"

She lifted her chin, water sluicing down. "There is no need for sarcasm."

He turned Cadeym, going slow now since the wet ground was quickly turning to mud, sucking at the horses hooves. If they weren't careful one of the horses could slip and injure itself.

They'd gone only about a half mile when the lass let out with a screech and slid to the ground, landing on her bum. Her horse threw its head, the saddle hanging on its side. Without looking back, the animal walked off, leaving her sitting on the ground.

"Oh!" She slapped the muddy ground with her fists, spraying mud over her shirt and face.

Biting the inside of his cheek to keep from laughing, Liam jumped from his horse and strode to where she sat. Anger flashed in her whiskey colored eyes as she glared up at him.

"Is there a problem, lass?"

"Don't you dare laugh! I've never fallen off a horse in my life. It must be these Scottish animals." She tried to push herself up, but her feet slid out from under her and she fell back down. Liam reached his hand out. Obviously not happy about accepting his help, she took hold of his hand nevertheless, and he pulled her up.

She placed her fists on her hips and gazed at the rear end of her horse making its way back to the dry, warm stable. "Now what do I do?"

"Well, lass, the only thing you can do is ride with me."

She looked at him aghast. "With you?"

"I imagine ye could wait here until a riderless horse ambles by, but it might be some time, and I'm anxious to get back to Dundas."

He tried very hard not to notice how her wet clothes clung to her body. He would never have expected this English miss to wear breeches and ride a horse astride. Despite her small size, the lass had plenty of curves under those wet garments. "Well what will it be, lass? We'll be drowning soon."

"Very well. I will ride with you," she said, none too graciously. She glared up at him, the water plopping onto her chest from her pert nose.

Where were all those fine English manners?

• • •

Before she could catch her breath, Liam wrapped his hands around her waist and hoisted her onto the horse. Within seconds, he was behind her and urging the horse forward. The rain continued to pelt them as they made their way back. She still couldn't believe she'd slid off the horse. No doubt the girth hadn't been tight enough, but she'd never made that mistake before.

"Why aren't you in a riding outfit, mounted on a side-saddle as a proper English miss?"

"Not that it is any of your concern, but I prefer breeches when I'm riding in the country. The freedom is wonderful. As a man, you have no idea how cumbersome a riding outfit is, and how awkward you must position yourself on a side saddle. All the women in my family ride this way when we're not in Town."

She held herself stiffly, not wanting to touch his body, which was indeed hard to ignore. The man was so large it was as if he surrounded her completely. His arms rested against hers as he held the reins and directed the horse. She began to shiver, the cold rain soaking to her skin through her clothes. Since she always left off her stays when she donned her outfit for riding, the chill seemed to go to her very bones.

"If you lean back against me, lass, you won't be so cold."

"I am fine, thank you." To belie her words, she only shook more. Goodness, the rain was cold. She was sure her lips were blue. The downpour continued, making her miserable.

"Ye will be throwing yourself to the ground again if you don't stop the shaking. Lean against me, and we can share the warmth."

She'd never been so cold in her life. Despite her misgivings, she eased back against Liam's chest, his body warm despite being as wet as hers. It was slow going with the rain and wind so fierce. This was not the soft rain of England, but a wild gale such as she had never seen. So fitting in the rugged beauty of the Highlands.

Sybil tried very hard to ignore the feel and smell of the man behind her. His warm breath teased the skin on the back of her neck, not doing much for her shivers. Her bottom was snug against an area of which a proper young lady never took notice. Had she been caught riding in this manner in London, she would be forced to marry the barbarian.

The miserable ride made conversation impossible, which was fine with her. She had nothing to say to the man, and only ached for the trip to come to an end so she could strip off all her wet clothes and climb into a hot bath. After having her lady's maid, Bessie, fix her a hot toddy, she would have a tray sent to her room so she could stay in bed. She would be lucky if she didn't catch a chill after this debacle.

They emerged from the wooded area surrounding the castle, and her spirits rose when the stable came into view. Sybil leaned forward, anxious now to be away from Liam and his enveloping warmth.

"Easy, lass. We're almost there, and ye don't want to slip again." His deep voice rolled over her, making her even more anxious to leave his presence. She didn't like the way he made her feel, and had no intention of examining why that was. They reached the stable, and she sighed with relief as he swung his leg over and dropped to the ground.

Without a word, he encircled her waist and pulled her off the horse. She rested her palms on his shoulders as he lifted her down, his muscles rippling under her hands as he moved his arms. Her mouth dried up, and her heart did a double beat as her eyes connected with his. His eyes grew wide, and he appeared as startled as she.

Good heavens, the last thing I want is to feel an attraction to a whiskey swilling, brawling, lustful Scot.

Chapter Two

The next morning Sybil entered the great hall for breakfast where one of the maids had directed her. The room was quite large, with an immense fireplace against one wall. Colorful and well maintained tapestries hung on the walls, blocking out the fierce Scotland winds. A small fire burned brightly, warming the area directly in front of it, where Lord Somerville, Duncan, and Liam sat breaking their fast. All three rose as she approached the long table.

"A surprise, my lady. I thought the ladies would all be abed this morning." Duncan pulled out a chair for her.

"I enjoy morning very much. Once the sun is up, I am unable to stay asleep." She took the platters passed to her from the men and filled her plate with eggs, sausage, some type of bread that resembled a scone, and cheese. She passed on the items she didn't recognize.

"I'm happy to see ye haven't had to take to yer bed with the ague," Liam said.

"Not at all. I can assure you I have a strong constitution, sir." She picked up her fork and regarded him. "What do I call you? My laird? My lord?"

He sat back and grinned at her. "Liam will do nicely." He eyed her plate. "Surely ye want some black pudding and porridge. And perhaps some haggis?" Liam's eyes danced with mirth. Did the man do nothing but tease?

"Thank you, but I have never tried haggis or black pudding, and porridge is not one of my favorite dishes."

"Ach, you must try it at least," Liam said, cutting a piece of the pudding and plopping it rudely onto her plate. The challenge in his eyes had her stiffening her shoulders. Whatever game the man was playing did not amuse her. Somehow she felt he was testing her mettle and was waiting for her to snap at him again, which he seemed to be expecting.

Conjuring up her sweetest smile, she cut a small piece of the pudding and put it into her mouth. The strong taste was not unpleasant. She tried another bite and found she actually liked it. "Very good."

Liam looked nonplussed at her, which made her grin. The man really was baiting her, and she'd disappointed him. This visit might be quite fun, after all. There was nothing she enjoyed more than sparring with a worthy opponent, and she believed Laird MacBride was indeed a laudable adversary. Even though he was a Scot.

The exchange made her ache once again for her twin. They'd had so many giggles over the years that perhaps matching swords with Liam could distract her.

"Once Lady Margaret and Lady Somerville are up and about, I thought we might take a ride into the village and visit the stores. I know ladies like to shop," Duncan said.

"And mayhaps we can take luncheon at the Maydenhead Inn." Liam added as he settled his napkin alongside his plate.

Sybil choked on the sausage she was eating, causing Liam to tap her between her shoulders. *Maidenhead Inn?* Leave it to the barbaric Scots to name an inn thus.

"Is something amiss, lass?" Liam's barely controlled laughter tightened her muscles. Had she not known better she would have sworn he'd made up that name merely to unsettle her. But this was Scotland. No doubt there would be such a place in the village.

She narrowed her eyes at him. "Not at all. A piece of sausage merely went the wrong way." Waving her hand in dismissal, she took a sip of tea.

The rest of the meal passed in pleasant conversation, but Sybil kept herself on alert for Liam's next attempt to test her. He'd thrown down the gauntlet, and she was more than prepared to pick it up. Matching wits with the Highlander could be quite entertaining.

Once the other ladies had arisen, the three of them and Lord Somerville entered the well-sprung carriage and headed to town. Liam and Duncan rode their horses, the weather having cleared since yesterday's storm. Bright sunlight beamed down on the group, the countryside freshened with the previous day's rain. Once again, Sybil was charmed by the beautiful countryside. As far as the eye could see, rolling hills of grass, dotted with sheep and snug little stone cottages gave the area an appearance of a carefully painted landscape. She had to admit the sight was truly beautiful. Too bad Scotland was inhabited by Scots.

As she gazed out the window, her view was suddenly blocked. Duncan and Liam rode next to the carriage. She studied Liam, the nearest to her. He certainly sat a horse well. His bulging thighs gripped the horse's side as he held the reins gently, allowing his legs to drive the animal. The two men were deep in conversation, which gave her the opportunity to study the rest of the man.

Despite the cooler weather, Liam rode with only a shirt, jacket, boots, and breeches. The wind plastered the jacket to his chest, outlining the man underneath. Today his hair was pulled back into a queue, tied with a ribbon. Her breath caught as his horse moved up farther and she got a glimpse of his backside. Heat rose in her face, and she quelled the urge to fan her cheeks.

Without warning, he turned his head and gazed directly into her eyes. He broke into a disarming smile and gave her a slight salute. Drat! He'd caught her staring again. Flustered, she drew herself up and leaned forward as if someone across from her were speaking. How embarrassing!

The village was delightful. A couple dozen shops, all connected together, lined both sides of the street. They passed a draper, milliner, dry goods, blacksmith, and boot maker. On the opposite side stood a small schoolhouse, a lovely stone church, and a rather large general store with a painted sign stating *Jennie Awthings*. At the very end of the street, up on a small hill, was *The Maydenhead Inn*. So he hadn't made the name up.

The carriage rolled to a stop in front of the milliner. Lord Somerville climbed out first, then turned to assist his wife and the other two ladies. Duncan and Liam tethered their horses and joined the group. "What shall it be first, ladies? Ribbons, hats, gloves?"

Lady Margaret and her mother opted to visit the milliner. Sybil elected to visit the bookstore between the church and schoolhouse.

"Bookstore, lass?" Liam's raised brows almost reached his hairline.

She eyed him coolly. "Yes. I do know how to read."

"I never doubted ye for a moment." He grinned at her. "Mayhap I'll join ye. 'Tis been a while since I've visited the bookstore."

She smiled sweetly. "Do you know which one it is, or do I need to read the shop's names for you?"

Liam burst out with laughter. "Nay, lass. I ken which one the bookstore is. 'Tis the one with the books in the window."

"How very clever, my laird."

"Liam," he responded. He extended his arm to Sybil, and she took it even though she didn't want to be so close to the Scot. Her stomach performed a small little ballet, and her breathing sped up. Perhaps she had caught a chill, after all. Her skin certainly felt flushed.

• • •

Liam held the door open to the bookstore, and Lady Sybil passed through. So far the lass had done everything counter to what he'd expected. Riding in pants, joining the men for an early breakfast, and now when the other ladies were inspecting ribbons and bows, this unusual Englishwoman was strolling the aisles of the bookstore.

"What are your favorite books?" Hands linked behind his back, Liam walked alongside her.

"I like novels. As well as books on history and geography."

"And what novels have ye found to your liking?"

She pulled a book from the shelf and turned to him. "Miss Jane Austen is probably the author whose novels I've read the most. I read *Pride and Prejudice* as well as her *Sense and Sensibility*."

"Ah, very fine stories."

Sybil's eyes widened. "You are familiar with Miss Austen's works?"

"Indeed I am. I have also read *Pride and Prejudice* as well as *Sense and Sensibility*." He loved the surprised look on the lass's face. No doubt she believed all Scotsmen to be barbaric illiterates. For now, he would keep his attendance at University of Edinburg to himself.

"I also enjoyed reading *Patronage* by Maria Edgeworth." He paused as her jaw dropped. "I believe Miss Edgeworth has a gift for expressing social mores by the use of clever dialog. And then, of course, there is Frances Burney's *The Wanderer*. A most interesting story of women's economic plight."

He leaned over and used his index finger to raise Sybil's chin to close her mouth. "Ye might catch a bug or two that way, lass."

She yanked her head back and smoothed her hair, almost knocking her hat off. "I must admit, I am a bit surprised at the types of books you are familiar with."

"So it seems."

They continued to wander the room, pulling random books, discussing their merits, Liam trying his best to disconcert her. Why he was interested in raising her opinion of him remained a question. What did he care what a frivolous Sassenach thought of him? Except Lady Sybil was no frivolous lass. And certainly quite different from what he believed all Englishwomen to be.

A bell sounded as the door of the bookstore opened. Duncan walked up to them. "We are ready for luncheon. The others have gone up to the inn. Are ye both finished?"

"Yes." Sybil smiled and lifted the two books she'd chosen and moved to the counter. After laying them down, she calculated the coins to pay for them. Liam followed her and paid for the three books he had selected.

• • •

It was a short walk through the village and up to the inn. The Maydenhead Inn. Despite its vulgar name, the inside was quite pleasant, and the smell of fresh bread and some type of stew filled the air. Not even realizing she was hungry, Sybil was embarrassed to hear her stomach making ravenous noises. She glanced sheepishly up at Liam and met his laughing eyes. Despite the discomfort at her unladylike display, she had to grin at his mirthful glance.

Then she chastised herself. She should not want to share books, surreptitious jokes, and hunger pangs with this man. She wanted to watch her best friend marry and then return to civilization. Maybe not all Scots were illiterate barbarians, but that didn't mean she and this Scot could develop a *tendre.* She distrusted Scots and just because this one could spew some fancy book titles hadn't changed her mind.

Then she wondered why she was trying so hard to convince herself of this.

"We have some tasty lamb stew today, along with bread fresh out of the oven." A plump red-faced woman wiped her hands on her apron as she spoke to the group.

"That sounds fine to me," Duncan said.

Everyone else nodded their agreement, and the woman hurried away. Sybil's stomach gave another growl, and she glanced around the table. Of course the only person who noticed was Liam, who grinned.

"All that strolling around the book store has strengthened yer appetite." He spoke softly enough that no one else heard him.

Sybil tried very hard to cast him a stern glance, but her sense of humor got the best of her and she chuckled. It was truly an embarrassment, but nothing she could control. Liam looked at her with something akin to approval when she shrugged at her latest *faux pas*.

"Good for ye, lass."

Why did she glow under his praise? She shifted in her seat, uncomfortable with the reactions she continued to have with this man.

"How are the wedding plans coming along, McKinnon?" Lord Somerville asked.

"Mrs. Galbraith tells me all is in order. The guests will begin arriving on the morrow, and everyone has been in a flutter getting things ready. I believe she has some activities planned for the visitors."

"Will there be a ball?" Margaret asked.

"Yes. I believe Mrs. Galbraith has one set for two nights hence. I'm sure you ladies will be thrilled at the social doings."

"Yes, I think a ball is just the thing," Lady Somerville said. "Do you do much entertaining, McKinnon?"

"Not since mum passed. She had all the contacts, but now that Margaret will soon be my lady wife, I expect she will want to rekindle friendships with the neighboring families."

Lady Somerville turned to Liam. "Tell us a bit about your home."

Sybil was disgusted with herself at how interested she was in his answer. Yet she leaned forward, wanting to hear what he had to say.

"Da died several years ago. My mum manages my home until such time as I take a wife. Having done so for years, she is most efficient, and things run smoothly. We do some entertaining, but less as the years go on since mum is more than ready to hand over the responsibilities."

Lady Somerville regarded him. "You are betrothed, then?"

"No, my lady. But if my mum had her way, I would be married and already filling the nursery with bairns."

Sybil felt a jolt of what she hoped was not jealousy. She did not care who this Scot took to wife. That was a role she would never covet, and indeed she'd run screaming from the room if he even suggested such a thing.

Satisfied that she'd straightened that out with herself, she smiled at Liam, thereby assuring him that she had no designs on his person—or his would-be nursery filled with bairns.

"Now that I am to be married soon, I am hoping my friend joins me in matrimony." Duncan slanted a look at Liam that Sybil was sure was meant to nudge him toward the altar.

She certainly wished a happy life to whatever woman the barbarian chose. Hopefully, the poor girl would know ahead of time that all he would do is swill whiskey, pick fights, and charm his way into numerous beds. Since that thought had nothing at all to do with her experience thus far with the man, it didn't sit quite well, but that was something she wasn't going to bother with. All Scots were the same, and therefore Liam would be, as well.

"And what of you, lass?" Liam asked. "Now that your friend is to be married, will you be joining her?"

Sybil's face heated at his impertinent question. No gentleman would ask such a thing. Ill-mannered lout! "I have no desire to seek matrimony until an acceptable gentleman presents himself." She emphasized *gentleman*, hoping the rude Scot would understand she did not find him of that ilk.

Her annoyance rose when Liam leaned near to her and said for her ears only, "Ach, lass, 'tis hoping I am that whatever *gentleman* presents himself to ye is fond of his lady wife riding about the countryside in breeches."

"That is none of your business," she snapped.

"Aye, I agree." He leaned back, giving her a thoughtful look. "And 'tis thankful I am of that."

Honestly, the man had no idea how to behave with a lady. If he was trying to vex her, then he succeeded. If only there was a way to avoid him for the rest of her time here. It would be a long two weeks.

• • •

Liam had no idea why he enjoyed riling the lass up. Right now, she was pretending to ignore him, but the high color in her cheeks said otherwise. Despite her somewhat different ways, she was still an English princess. He best leave her be, get through the next days, and be on his way.

His mum would be all fired up for sure when he returned—wanting him to seek a bride and give her some bairns to spoil. And it was time. At thirty and one and laird of his clan, his responsibility was to marry and produce children. He kenned that, and fully intended to see to his duty. A good, strong Scottish lass for him. The only thing holding him back was a lack of candidates that held appeal.

No matter how many lasses his mum put in his path, there was not a one he wanted to look at for the rest of his life. His glance slid in Lady Sybil's direction. Despite her small size, she was a beauty. Clear skin, sparkling eyes, a full woman's body, and silky hair that he would love to release from its bindings and run his fingers through. As testy as the lass was, he kenned she would be a passionate bed partner. He could teach her all the things that would have her moaning under him, begging for release. At the image his thoughts portrayed, he began to harden and grow, shifting in his chair to accommodate his erection.

Lady Sybil threw her head back and laughed at something Lady Margaret said. No simpering, ladylike giggle, but a full husky laugh that exposed the creamy skin of her neck. He would love to place his lips on that very spot and feather the area with kisses. Then he would run his palms up the sides of her body, cupping her generous breasts, circling her nipples with his thumbs, hardening them into tight little peaks.

He mentally shook himself before he let out a groan. The woman of his fantasy looked over at him, her eyebrows raised. Had he made a sound that hinted at his thoughts? The temperature in the room rose, and no matter how much he moved about, he was uncomfortable sitting.

It would be a long two weeks.

Chapter Three

The evening of the much-anticipated ball had arrived. In addition to the few dozen visitors that were staying at Dundas for the wedding, much of the local gentry and clan had been invited, making for more than a hundred guests to crowd into the ballroom. Sybil entered the large room dressed in a pale blue soft muslin gown, with dark blue embroidery at the hem, under the bust and on the edges of the long sleeves. She wore her favorite pearls and matching ear bobs. Bessie had gathered her mass of brown wavy hair at her crown, with curls falling down her back, woven with pale blue satin ribbons.

She scanned the room, looking for Margaret amongst all the finery of the ladies and gentlemen. She rose on her tip-toes just as a deep male voice whispered in her ear. "It would appear being a wee lass has its disadvantages."

Lord, she hated how her stomach went all aflutter and her heartbeat sped up at the sound of the man's voice. And more disturbing was his scent drifting to her nostrils. Man, leather, and something spicy.

She turned to the Scot and answered in a cool voice. "Not everyone appreciates being a giant."

His booming laugh rang out, causing those in the general area to turn toward them. Liam extended his arm toward her and said, "Allow me to escort ye around the room so ye can find whoever it 'tis ye are so anxious to meet up with."

Sybil accepted his arm, reminded once again of the man's strength. His muscles were tight as a drum under her hand. "I was merely looking for Lady Margaret. She came down before I was ready."

"Ach, I saw the lovely lass a few minutes ago, holding very carefully onto The McKinnon's arm, surrounded by well-wishers." He glanced at her as the music started up. "Would ye honor me with a dance, lass?"

She should really stay far away from this man, given how she reacted to him, but there was no way to refuse without appearing rude. She stared into his mirthful eyes, wondering if he ever had a serious moment. "Yes, I would—lad."

Again that resounding laugh that drew attention from those close by. He tugged her close to his body, much too near, as far as she was concerned, and led her to the row of dancers. For a large man, he was graceful and an excellent dancer. His broad shoulders blocked out the rest of the room, so all she could see was his dark evening jacket, white waistcoat, and a neck cloth tied in a manner that would pass the toughest scrutiny in a London ballroom.

Except for his ginger colored hair, drawn away from his face once more, and tied with a ribbon at his nape, he could easily pass for an English gentleman. However, his size would still stand out. She'd never seen a man as overpowering as the Scot.

As they moved into a turn, he pulled her closer until she felt the strong muscles of his legs much too close to hers. The heat from his body warmed her, reminding her that he danced indecently near. She attempted to pull back, but he held her firm. "'Tis much too crowded, lass. Ye almost bumped into another dancer. Mayhap when the number ends we should take a stroll in the garden."

The last thing she wanted was to spend time in a dark garden with this man who confused her so. Being a Scot, he most likely wanted to dally with her—see how far she would let him go. She raised her chin and looked him in the eye. "I will not be strolling with you in the dark garden."

"Ye wound me, lass. Surely ye dinna think I would take advantage of ye?"

"That is precisely what I think."

He actually looked wounded, and she almost laughed out loud. As if he thought she was innocent enough not to know what a stroll in a dark garden meant. She hadn't survived four seasons in London without learning some things.

His lively eyes continued to stare at her until she grew uncomfortable. "Ach, mayhap you're right, lass. A walk in the garden is not a good idea."

The music finished, and Sybil curtsied to her partner and turned to continue looking for Margaret. To her annoyance, Liam stayed by her side, although truth be told, his size cleared a path for them much faster than she would have been able to do by herself.

"Lady Sybil, is that you?"

She turned to see Lord Warwick making his way through the crowd toward her. Her stomach tightened, remembering the last time she'd seen him in London. He'd been quite anxious for her to accept his suit, but she felt nothing for the man except slight friendship. That hadn't stopped him, however, from trying to compromise her at the Kennedy ball.

In addition, she'd heard he had run through his inheritance and was actively looking for a wife with a substantial dowry. No doubt so he could continue with his wastrel ways. Even if she did feel differently about him, she had no plans to be any man's bank account.

"My lord, how pleasant to see you." She offered her hand, attempting a smile.

He took her hand and kissed the air above it, moving closer to her than she would have liked. She backed up and stepped on Liam's foot. Turning to him, she said, "May I present David, Marquess of Warwick?" She paused and added, "and this, my lord, is Laird Liam MacBride."

The men nodded briefly and eyed each other like two animals in a cage about to pounce on a piece of meat between them. Sybil mentally rolled her eyes at the performance. Honestly, neither man had a claim on her, so all their affectation was for naught. It was a problem she and Sarah had encountered many times during their Season.

"What brings you to Dundas, my lord?" Sybil asked.

"The McKinnon is related to my mother in some way." He waved a careless hand. "Not sure exactly how it all works, but I didn't want to pass up the opportunity to flee London and get some fresh air."

More likely he was fleeing his creditors, but Sybil merely smiled.

"And you?"

"Lady Margaret is a close friend. I traveled with her and her parents a few days ago." Either the crowd was increasing or Warwick was having trouble staying on his feet because he leaned even closer, forcing her to move so that her back practically rested on Liam's chest.

The odor of strong spirits on his breath made the closeness between them more unbearable.

"I believe it is becoming quite crowded. Perhaps we should move to the terrace." Warwick leered at her, but she reached for Liam as he immediately extended his arm.

Liam lowered his head and spoke softly. "Mayhap a stroll in the garden is not such a bad idea, after all, lass?"

Although she narrowed her eyes at him, she was grateful for his presence. She didn't trust Warwick and certainly didn't want to have him that close to her. At least in the garden she could maintain her distance from the man.

• • •

Liam was not at all happy about the man who hovered over Sybil, obviously making her uncomfortable. Another London dandy. But the lass's wariness was real, not just distaste for the man. The three of them headed to the terrace, maneuvering their way through the crowd.

Never one to enjoy a room full to bursting with people, he was only too happy to leave the noise and heat behind. Just as he reached for the door to escort Sybil through, a tap on his shoulder had him turning around.

"MacBride, a word please?" Mr. Patrick Wollsley, a local horse breeder, stepped in front of the trio, blocking the doorway. A man of small stature, it was hard for Liam to accept that the man was Scottish. But his horses were fine horseflesh, and he'd acquired several strong animals from him in the past.

"I will escort Lady Sybil outside." Warwick quickly shifted her arm from Liam's to his own. "She seems to be in need of fresh air."

Liam scowled at him, especially after the panicked look the lass sent him. "Mayhap we can speak another time?" he asked Wollsley.

"'Twill only take a moment. I have a fine stallion I think ye might be interested in. 'Tis one ye asked about before."

Before Liam could gracefully offer to speak with him later, Warwick had the lass out the door, and headed toward the gardens. Frustrated, but unable to do much, Liam turned back to Wollsley. "Be verra quick. I've something I need to see to."

Liam's mind wandered as Wollsley blathered on about the stallion, and what a fine stud he would make in Liam's stables. Why would the lass look so anxious when Warwick whisked her away? Surely the man wouldn't attempt to dishonor her in any way?

His agitation grew in direct proportion to Wollsley's praise of the animal, marking all of the stud's finer points and abilities. Finally, unable to bear any more, Liam interrupted the man. "Once I am back at Bedlay Castle I will send for ye to bring the animal to me."

Wollsley nodded vigorously. "Verra good, Laird."

Liam shook the man's hand and headed toward the door. He stepped outside, the night air cool, typical for a Scottish May evening. The moon cast a faint light over the area, slightly illuminating a few couples deep in conversation. He took note that none of them was a slight Englishwoman in a blue gown. He wandered down the few steps leading to the garden pathway with winding lanes of bluebells and wild hyacinths. Interspersed with oak, birches, and mountain ash trees, were the magnificent colors of rhododendrons and azaleas.

But little of the spectacular glory of the flowers and trees provided a distraction to his search for Lady Sybil. His muscles tightened as he rounded a bend of Scottish primrose to see her shoved up against a tree while she fought off Warwick's advances. The man had one hand on her breast and his knee wedged between her legs. His mouth covered hers, and she appeared to be trying to move her head, but to no avail. She pushed at his chest, but her slight size would never move the man.

But Liam could. With a roar as fierce as any animal, he grabbed Warwick by his shoulders and wrenched him away from Lady Sybil. He tossed the blackguard to the ground, then lifted him up by his neck and slammed his fist in his nose. A satisfying crunch had Warwick crying out as he collapsed.

Panting more from anger than effort, he snarled at the man. "I suggest ye find yerself a vehicle to carry ye back to London. I will be more than happy to convey yer regrets to the bride and groom." Liam dusted his hands and straightened his jacket before turning to Lady Sybil.

She stared down at Warwick, her eyes wide, tears leaking from their depths. Her shaky hands covered her mouth. Liam enfolded her in his arms "'Tis all right, lass. 'Tis over now. He won't hurt ye again."

Sybil continued to shake, her entire body trembling. Liam held her closer, stroking her back as he leaned his chin on the lass's head, the scent of her hair softening parts of him while hardening others. For all her spirit, the lass was terrified. Her crying turned to soft sobs. Realizing how bad it would look should anyone stumble upon them, he placed his hands on her shoulders and eased her back. One look at her and rage swept through him.

The top of her bodice was wrinkled in such a way that it was obvious she'd been roughly handled. Her hair fell about her shoulders in disarray, her eyes swollen from tears. But unlike what he'd expected, the lass had not swooned, and right now her eyes flashed with anger.

"I wish you had broken his nose," she snapped.

Liam winked at her. "I think I did."

Warwick had scurried away while Liam had been comforting the lass. After seeing the condition of Lady Sybil, 'twas a good thing he had, or Liam would have been more than happy to break something else on the scoondrel's body.

"Lass, I'm afraid ye can't be going back into the ball like that. 'Tis best if I escort ye up to yer bedchamber to change yer clothes."

She shook her head and brushed the front of her gown. "No. I have no wish to return to the ball. I shall seek my room and retire." Seeming to pull herself together, she lifted her chin and asked, "Are you aware of another way to the floor with the bedchambers?"

Liam took her arm. "I am. I spent many a summer here when I was a lad. Duncan and I kenned how to slip in and out of the place without disturbing his mum and da, if ye get my meaning."

Despite her tension, Lady Sybil smiled warmly at him, once again gainsaying his notion of how an English miss behaved. She should be wailing and complaining. Instead, she accepted his arm and they carefully picked their way through the dark to the back door of the castle, almost as if they were on an adventure.

"'Tis best if ye follow behind me, lass." He took her hand in his and opened the heavy door. "Stay near, and dinna say a word."

They slipped through the portal. Once the door closed behind them, the scant moonlight disappeared, casting them into total darkness. Behind him the lass gasped, and he tightened his hold on her hand to reassure her.

They eased their way up the stairs, the noise of the kitchen staff scurrying around under their feet as they climbed. With everyone busy, hopefully, they would not meet anyone before they reached her chamber. Once they gained the second floor, Liam preceded Sybil down the corridor then turned to her. "Which room is yers, lass?"

"It is hard for me to say. Usually I carry a candle up the stairs. From the other end of the corridor it is the third door on the left hand side."

He nodded and moved them forward. The sound of voices came from the direction they were headed. Liam stopped and pushed Sybil behind him. The sound grew louder, a man and woman speaking in whispers, the woman giggling as they moved along. Liam opened the door where they stood and ushered Sybil in.

"What are you doing? This is not my chamber."

"Nay, lass. I realize that, but if we stayed where we were 'tis likely we would interrupt a private meeting."

"What do you mean, a private meeting? Now?"

Moonlight drifted through the small window, highlighting

Sybil's brown hair with hints of gold, cascading down around her slender shoulders. Her wide light brown eyes regarded him with innocence. Did she truly not understand what he'd just told her?

"'Tis a man and woman, lass."

Her mouth formed a perfect circle and she blinked several times. "Oh. That sort of a meeting."

"Aye. That sort of a meeting."

"Well, what will we do now? We can't stay in here all night."

"They were headed to one of the rooms. As soon as we hear a door latch close, we can proceed."

She shivered, the room being chilly, and her gown not covering much of her upper body. Liam tugged her to him, and wrapped his arms around her, which was a mistake. In his attempt to warm the lass, he was treated to the scent of lavender drifting up to tease his nostrils. The softness of her breasts pressed against his chest, and the warmth of her body had him thinking of what the couple they'd stumbled upon would be enjoying verra shortly.

"Are they still in the corridor?" Sybil's voice seemed strained. Could she be as affected by their closeness as he was?

He released his hold on her and pressed his ear to the door. All was silent. Sybil rubbed her palms up and down her arms. The lass was cold, and he needed to get her to her room and a fire started to warm her.

"I believe they've found a place for their meeting."

"Very funny."

He eased the door open and pulled her out. Grasping her hand in his, they continued on until they reached her door. He opened it and they slipped inside.

"You can't come in here! If we get caught it will be a disaster."

"Ye are in need of some warmth. I will start a fire for ye, and then leave ye in peace."

"Well, please hurry. My maid or someone could come into the room."

"Ach, that would be a problem, in truth. Sit yerself over there on the bed and I will have the room warm in no time."

Her shivering grew worse as he broke up the peat and used a flint to start the fire. Once he had a small flame, he stood and removed his jacket. Crossing the room, he wrapped the jacket around Sybil.

"Thank you," she whispered, looking up at him with soulful eyes. By the heavens, the lass was a beauty. And much stronger than he'd given her credit for. He turned on his heel and returned to the fireplace, adding another peat block. He dinna need to be spending time in the lass's bedchamber. He squatted in front of the fire, suddenly aware that she'd walked up behind him. She knelt and regarded him. "Thank you for tonight."

He poked at the block with a fire iron and shrugged his shoulders. "'Twas nothing."

She touched his arm. "Yes, it was something. Warwick tried the same thing at a ball in London. Luckily, my brother intervened and a scandal was avoided."

"I'm sorry I let ye go outside with the man."

"You had no way of knowing."

He dropped the fire iron and turned to her, running the backs of his fingers over her soft cheek. "Aye, I saw the fear in yer face. I never should have stopped to speak with Wollsley."

"It is over now." She licked her lips, the action sending all his blood to his groin. If he dinna leave soon he would do something he would curse himself for in the morning.

"Aye. The fire is burning brightly, so 'tis time for me to leave." He rose and extended his hand. She stared at it for moment, then took his hand in hers. He pulled her up and drew her close. In the glow of the fireplace she bent her head back to stare in his eyes. She leaned toward him, and without thought, he lowered his head and took her lips in a soft kiss.

Her mouth was warm and moist. Like fine honey. His lips left hers to nibble at her earlobe. "Ach lass, 'tis such a temptation ye are."

No sooner had his whispered words left his mouth than she pulled back, her chest heaving. She backed away, her arms wrapped around her body and turned toward the fire. "You must go. We cannot do this."

"Aye. Ye are right." He ran his fingers through his hair. "Good night, lass."

When she didn't respond, he withdrew and turned to leave. He strode across the room and opened the door, checking to make sure the corridor was empty. He glanced over his shoulder, his last glimpse of her standing in front of the fire, staring at the flames. A beauty surrounded by an orange glow.

Chapter Four

The next morning the seven men eating breakfast stood as Sybil entered the great hall. It was a bit disconcerting to always be the only woman at breakfast. She really should be more like the other ladies and have toast and tea brought to her room each morning, but she was too restless and too anxious to see what the day would bring to languish in bed.

Liam drew a chair out for her. "Good morning, lass."

She nodded her thanks and reached for the teapot. Did he feel as uncomfortable about last night's kiss as she did? After she had climbed into bed, she'd tossed and turned for a couple of hours, the episode with Warwick barely a wisp of a thought compared to what had followed. Laird MacBride knew how to kiss. Extremely well.

"It appears Lord Warwick has been called away for a family emergency. He left early this morning." Liam stared at her straight-faced as he imparted the news.

Sybil hoped the flush she felt in her chest didn't reach

her face. "A shame. I hope everything is all right."

"I am sure whatever the emergency is, his being in London will benefit."

Only years of good breeding kept her from spewing out a mouthful of tea at Liam's casual remark. Yet he still looked as innocent as a babe. Another reason not to trust the man. He hid his feelings well. Most likely years of seducing women into his bed had sharpened his subterfuge skills. That was something she needed to remember, especially in light of last night's kiss.

"Lady Sybil, why is it ye are the only lady who enjoys breakfast?" Duncan eyed her full plate, a slight smile on his face.

She'd always had a good appetite and had never employed the ruse of eating like a bird when around gentlemen and then gorging oneself when alone. "I enjoy all of my meals. I'm afraid I have been cursed with an unladylike appetite."

"'Tis not unladylike, lass. 'Tis a blessing to have a strong constitution. Most Englishwomen do not," Liam said.

She glanced at him, her eyebrows raised. "And you are so familiar with Englishwomen?"

Liam flushed, looking as though he wished to call back his words. Since her arrival at Dundas, several comments Liam had made indicated his idea of a typical Englishwoman was anything but complimentary. No doubt he thought them all weeping, swooning, fragile flowers. Truth be told, many of her acquaintances certainly fit that description, however, she and her sisters had always enjoyed an active, robust life.

"Nay, lass. But aside from yerself, the ones I have met seem a bit on the willow side compared to Scottish lasses."

"Hopefully, ye don't mean to include my betrothed in that statement, MacBride?" Duncan said.

"Ach, 'tis a lot of trouble my tongue is getting me into today. Mayhap I'll take a ride in the fresh air to settle my brain." He stood and turned to Duncan "Nay, Lady Margaret is a charming Englishwoman."

He was a few feet from the door when he turned and strode back to the table, standing in front of Sybil. "My lady, would ye care to join me in a ride?"

Surprised at not being addressed as "lass" which he'd done since he'd met her, she replied, "Yes, I would." She wiped her mouth on a napkin and stood. "I won't be long to change."

"Verra well, I will see to the horses."

Sybil hurried up the stairs to her bedchamber. Fortunately, Bessie was in her room when she arrived. "Oh, I'm glad you're here. Please unfasten me and pull out my breeches from my trunk."

"Breeches, my lady?" Bessie *tsked*, but did as she was bid. "What will these people think to see a fine English lady riding about in breeches?"

"I do it all the time at home, Bessie, you know that."

"Yes, but what will the Scots think?

Sybil fastened the buttons on her shirt as Bessie tied the back of her specially made breeches. "Laird MacBride has already seen me in my breeches." She turned, finding it hard to keep the smile off her face. "He wasn't shocked. Well, perhaps a bit. But I got the impression I had risen in his regard."

Sybil took one last glance in the mirror and pinched her cheeks. Then she chastised herself all the way to the stables. Laird MacBride was not someone she wished to impress. Despite rescuing her last night from Warwick and sneaking her into the house, then kissing her senseless, he was still a Scot with all the bad habits of that breed.

Didn't I just chastise him for thinking all Englishwomen were the same?

She pushed that uncomfortable thought to the back of her mind and entered the stable. In the dim light Liam stood next to the black stallion he'd ridden the other day, rubbing his large palm down the horse's velvety, soft nose. He murmured words in a language she didn't understand, most likely Gaelic.

The melodious rhythm of his words washed over her, tightening her nipples and moistening her woman's parts. What would it be like to have him stroke her bare skin like that and murmur Gaelic words into her ear? Mesmerized, she watched him, his entire focus on the animal. Another ploy he most likely engaged to woo a woman into bed.

As an unmarried miss she shouldn't even be aware of such things. However, Sybil and Sarah had discovered her brother Drake's hidden naughty book, and had spent many an evening in their bed commenting and giggling over the pictures. They had been amused to discover their older sisters, Marion and Abigail, had done the same thing. Except they'd been caught and sermonized by their brother.

Liam stood in front of the window where dust motes danced in a stream of sunlight. He presented a virile image, one any woman would appreciate. With golden highlights in his ginger-colored hair and strong features—those of a warrior in times past—his countenance was remarkable. Enough so that her mouth dried up and tiny muscles fluttered low in her belly. Her eyes drifted downward to his broad shoulders covered in a white lawn shirt tucked into tight breeches. His muscular thighs were massive, as wide as her waistline. And his bottom!

"Have ye had enough time to admire me, lass?" His deep, chiding voice broke into her thoughts, causing heat to rise to her face which, no doubt, was now crimson.

She raised her chin and assessed him coolly. "You think quite a bit of yourself, sir. I was merely admiring the horse."

He broke into a grin and dropped his hand from the animal. "Verra good, lass. I like a woman who can think fast."

"I'm sure I have no idea what you are talking about." She swept past him—not so effective in breeches—and approached the other horse that had been tacked. Murmuring to the animal until she could collect her composure, she asked, "What is his name?"

"Acair."

She continued to brush her palm over Acair's nose. He was a beauty, dark brown with white stockings.

"If yer ready, lass, we can set off."

Before she could move a muscle, Liam's hands were wrapped around her waist, and she was hoisted onto the saddle. "I can mount myself."

"'Tis sure I am ye can, but mounting has always been my favorite part of the ride."

Once again heat flooded her body and rose to her face. She snapped her head around, but he stared at her in all innocence. *Ha! He was as innocent as a wolf.*

Without further conversation, he moved to his horse and threw his leg over the saddle and grabbed the reins. She headed out of the stable before him, not so sure she liked the view of her bottom she gave him. She pulled up on her reins to allow him to catch up. If there was to be any gawking at bottoms, it would be her peering at his.

Damn the man for making me think things most improper

for a lady.

• • •

Once they reached the open field past the wooded area surrounding the castle, they gave the horses their head. The wind whipped the tie from Liam's hair, allowing it to blow free. The cool air on his face felt wonderful, reminding him why he loved the Highlands so much. The dandies could keep their London ballrooms and smelly, hot city. Give him fresh air and beautiful scenery any time.

The lass had no trouble keeping up with him, and a quick glance in her direction told him she was enjoying the ride as much as he. Her hair ribbon too, had come loose and the silky strands of her locks streamed behind her. She turned in his direction, a huge grin on her face, her cheeks rosy from the ride. Her breasts rose and fell with her deep breaths, hardening him in places that would make the ride uncomfortable if he continued to dwell on her.

They climbed several hills until they came to his favorite spot. Pulling on the reins, he brought the horse to a trot, then a walk. Sybil did the same. They rode for a while until the horses had cooled down, then Liam brought his horse to a stop. Pointing toward the north, he said, "Ye see the castle in the distance, on the fourth hill?"

Sybil raised her hand to her forehead to block the sun. "Yes. I see it."

"'Tis my home, Bedlay Castle. It sets inland about a half mile from the North Sea."

"Yes. You've said you and Duncan are neighbors."

"Aye. We spent many weeks together when we were

lads."

Leaning back in her saddle, she regarded him, her lively eyes filled with curiosity. "Tell me some more about your family."

Liam rested his hands on his thighs and stared off over the verdant hills and valleys, toward his home. "My mum and da were both grandchildren of clans that went through the Jacobite revolution and the Clearances that followed. Made for a strong dislike of the Sassenach."

"Ah. You mean me."

He grinned at her affronted posture. "Aye." Truth be told, the time spent with the lass had not proven the things he'd accepted as fact most of his life. Sybil was far from an English princess. All the women here, with the exception of Sybil, Lady Margaret, and Lady Somerville, were Scottish. Yet the lass was the only one who appeared at breakfast each morn, rode the hills in breeches, and hadn't picked up an embroidery needle since she'd arrived.

"Do you have siblings?"

He warmed at the thought of the minxes. "Aye. I have two sisters. Catriona is three and ten, no longer a wee lass. Alanna is two years her senior."

"That is quite a gap between you and your sisters. I assume you are much older?"

"I reached my thirty-first year this past winter. Da wanted more sons, so he kept mum busy, but she lost so many bairns." He shook his head. "Catriona near killed her."

"And your parents?"

"Da passed away soon after Catriona's birth. Mum still controls Bedlay, but reminds me every day of my duty to marry and fill the nursery with bairns." He grinned at her.

"She keeps inviting lasses to sup with us. Sometimes I find myself tripping over them."

Sybil laughed—that deep, throaty laugh—so strange in such a wee lass. Although this wee lass had plenty of curves a man could wrap his hands around. "Now that I've confessed all, tell me about yer family."

"My father died rather suddenly a few years ago." She paused, a sheen of tears in her lovely eyes.

"You were close?"

"Yes. He was right there in the middle of our large, noisy family one minute, and dead from a broken neck the next." Her throat worked as she tried to control her emotions, blinking rapidly to clear her eyes of tears. "My brother is the Duke of Manchester." She shifted on her saddle to turn to him, a grin on her face. "He is married to a American botanist! Can you imagine? And he allows her to work in her science."

"Very forward thinking."

"Oh, it wasn't easy. He gave her a difficult time in the beginning." She grinned, apparently amused at some memories. "I also have four sisters."

"Ach, indeed a large family."

She nodded. "There's my sister Marion, married to a baron—who is blind. My sister Abigail is married to a rector, my twin sister Sarah, and the last of our brood, Mary, are still unmarried." She glanced at him, mirth in her eyes. "As am I."

"'Tis glad I am to hear it since ye responded so well to my kiss." He loved the red flush that crept up from her neck to her lovely cheeks. "A twin are ye?"

"Yes. This is the first time in my life I'm away from her. It seems strange somehow, and freeing at the same time."

"Freeing in what way?"

"As much as I love Sarah, we have been treated like a matching set our entire lives. Shared birthday parties, shared come-outs, shared friends, shared everything." She sighed and continued. "When we both received a strand of pearls for our sixteenth birthday I begged my father to return them to the jeweler and replace them with a golden pendant. I love pearls, but I just wanted something different from my twin."

A ducal brother married to a scientist and a sister married to a rector. A father willing to return an expensive piece of jewelry to please a daughter who just wanted to feel apart from her twin. Indeed, not only was the lass dissimilar from his idea of English, but she apparently came from an entire family of nonconformists.

"Ye appear to have a verra different family than what I've been told about the English."

"As much as I would like to say all your assumptions about the English are wrong, I must admit, my family is a bit different. When we were young, my mother actually got down on the floor and played with us." Apparently warming to the subject of her family, she continued. "We spent most of our childhood in the country. Mother felt the London air was not good for our lungs. That gave us quite a bit of freedom."

"And that is where you learned to ride in men's breeches?"

She nodded. "As do my sisters. Father had them specially made for us. Well, except for Marion." She wrinkled her forehead. "She is too much of a lady."

Liam threw back his head and laughed. He couldn't remember when he'd found a lass so entertaining. The women his mother paraded before him were only interested in his money and lands. They spoke of nothing except how they would redecorate Bedlay Castle, not caring that he found it quite pleasant just the way it was. And the lasses his mum would not consider worthy as mother to her grandchildren were more interested in what was between his legs. Not that he objected to those lasses, since a man had needs. But he didn't seek them out for conversation.

This one was different. She never even hinted about his land or money. Although a wee lass, she was strong and confident. Just thinking about the smooth, silky skin under those breeches wreaked havoc with his blood supply. "Have ye had contact with many Scots, lass?"

"No. But like you, I held notions of what Scotsmen were like. My mother's aunt married a Scotsman. A large man who favored drink and found it very difficult to find his way to her bed. Yet he had no trouble finding beds of other ladies," she said. "I know that infidelity is accepted in my world, but he was not discreet, and it humiliated my aunt."

"But your parents were discreet?"

"No!" She pulled herself up and glared at him. "They had no need to be discreet. My parents adored each other. They would never think of doing such a thing."

"Another way your family differs from the rest."

"It is one reason why my brother bemoans the responsibility of his sisters. None of us will marry for any reason other than love. We all feel we deserve what my parents had."

"And have they succeeded?"

"My siblings? Yes. A couple didn't start off that way, but all have extremely happy marriages with devoted spouses."

They both sat, their thoughts keeping them occupied. The sun disappeared behind a cloud, causing Sybil to shiver.

"We best be getting back." Liam glanced at the gathering

clouds. "I dinna wish to get caught in another storm."

The ride back to Dundas was quiet, each of them occupied with their thoughts. How different the lass and her family were from what he'd held as the truth. He quickly pushed away the thought that kept nudging at him.

If I can change my mind about the English, what would it take to change Sybil's idea of Scots? And do I want to?

Chapter Five

"Come," Sybil called at the tap on her bedchamber door.

It was the day after her ride with Liam. They'd spent the rest of the day in indoor pursuits since the storm that had threatened had arrived with a vengeance shortly after luncheon. The men had gathered in the library doing whatever it was men did when they gathered, and the ladies had taken to the drawing room, with Lady Boswick, Duncan's aged aunt, acting as hostess.

"Since the weather has cleared, we are going on a picnic today!" Margaret said excitedly as she danced into Sybil's room. "Cook is fixing several baskets and all the young ladies and gentlemen will ride in wagons to the picnic site. Isn't that wonderful? I've never ridden in a wagon before."

"That sounds like fun. In that case, I will wear one of my older dresses." Sybil reached into her trunk and after pawing through the contents, pulled out a heavier brown muslin gown.

"Why? We will have tables and chairs. The servants are bringing them out and setting them up now."

Sybil laughed. "You know me better than that. I don't plan to sit prettily when I can be investigating all the beautiful woods." She turned and held her hair up so Margaret could undo her buttons.

"Although we are the best of friends, I will never understand you, Sybil."

Shrugging out of her gown, she slipped the other one over her head and wiggled until it fell into place. "You seemed quite at home yesterday afternoon in the drawing room. What do you think of Lady Boswick?"

"Scary, at first." Margaret's fingers worked to fasten the buttons. "But after she ordered me to sit near her and we talked at length, I found her to be gruff only on the outside."

Sybil turned and grasped Margaret's shoulders. "Are you truly happy? Will Duncan be a worthy husband to you?"

"I must admit I was a bit frightened when we arrived, but Duncan has been remarkable. He has done everything to make me feel at home. I think this may be a very pleasant marriage."

Pleasant.

While she was happy for Margaret, Sybil wanted no part of a "pleasant" marriage. She desired passion and love. Marriage to a man who could stir her emotions, make her enjoy the pleasures of the marriage bed. She'd seen the looks her sisters gave their husbands, and her brother his wife. That is what she wanted—a connection that linked two people, as if no one else in the world existed. A man who would become part of her very soul.

A man like Liam.

Good Lord where did that thought come from?

• • •

Four wagons filled with excited guests rolled slowly over the hill. The sun was strong and had already dried up most of the moisture from yesterday's storm. Unlike the Englishwomen who all carried parasols to protect their skin, the Scottish ladies enjoyed the warmth from the infrequent sun on their faces.

The gentlemen were in two wagons and the ladies in the other two. The picnickers shouted back and forth about the games they would play, who would be on whose team, and which teams would likely win. One Scottish woman in particular, Moira Crawford, as she was introduced to Sybil, spent most of the ride bantering back and forth with Liam.

She'd arrived last evening with her parents, and first thing this morning she'd latched onto Liam and held on like a dog with a bone. Not that Sybil cared or even noticed. It was just that she felt sorry for the woman making such a cake of herself. But Liam seemed to be enjoying himself with the tart, so who was she to complain?

The wagons rolled to a stop, and the gentlemen hopped down, hurrying to the ladies' wagons to assist them. Liam came to stand directly in front of Sybil, who was almost nudged off her feet by Moira. "My Laird, 'tis so grateful I am to have such strong arms to lift me down," the girl whimpered.

Regaining her balance, Sybil snorted and took the hand of Mr. Pennyworth, another guest who reached for her. Once the ladies had all been helped out of the conveyances, they strolled in groups to where the servants had set up tables and chairs. Mr. Pennyworth held onto Sybil's arm as they made their way up the slight hill.

He was a pleasant man, a Scot, but nowhere near as broad or tall as Duncan and Liam. Perhaps not all Scotsmen were giants. Mr. Pennyworth blathered on about something, which prevented her from hearing what Liam and Miss Crawford were talking about. Whatever it was, Liam leaned closer to the chit so he could hear her. Honestly, did he have to be so gullible? Of course the girl purposely spoke softly so he would have to bend his head closer to her. Men were such fools.

She turned to Mr. Pennyworth, flashing him a brilliant smile. The man stumbled and stopped speaking. He seemed to have a problem regaining his thoughts, which made it possible for her to hear Liam's chuckle. She turned her head to see him peering at her with amusement. Did he think she purposely smiled at Mr. Pennyworth because she was jealous of Miss Crawford? What a ridiculous notion. As if she cared who Liam let fawn all over him.

"May I escort you to a chair, Lady Sybil?" Mr. Pennyworth viewed her with such a lovesick expression she felt as if she should pat him on the head like a devoted puppy.

"Yes, thank you."

Sybil found herself directly across from Liam and Miss Crawford.

"Lady Sybil isn't this wonderful?" Miss Crawford's very young eyes shone bright with excitement. "There is going to be a scavenger hunt."

Sybil smiled brightly at the young woman. "Yes. Extremely exciting! I'm having a hard time keeping my aged heartbeat steady."

Liam was taken with a fit of coughing that Sybil took great effort to ignore.

"The Laird and I are going to be partners," Miss Crawford panted.

"Indeed? How very thrilling for you both." Sybil turned to Mr. Pennyworth. "Would you like to take a stroll?"

The man jumped up so quickly he knocked his chair over. Red-faced, he picked up the chair and extended his arm to Sybil. She raised her chin and took his arm.

"Enjoy your stroll, lass," Liam threw out as they sauntered off.

Sybil dipped her head in acknowledgment and continued on as Mr. Pennyworth blathered about some nonsense.

• • •

Liam watched Sybil stroll away, clinging to the arm of the wee man, her hips swaying delightfully. If he didn't ken better, it was almost as if she was jealous of his attention to Miss Crawford. Which was foolish since he'd been trying to avoid the young lass all morning. Her constant chatter grated on his nerves, and she had a habit of speaking so softly he had to lean down to hear what she had to say. Rarely had he found it worth the effort.

"Oh, Lady Sybil and Mr. Pennyworth, don't walk off. We will start the scavenger hunt very soon," Lady Margaret called. "I believe luncheon is ready?" she asked Lady Boswick.

The older woman nodded her agreement. "Yes, my dear. All ready."

Sybil and Pennyworth headed back to the tables and settled in the seats they'd just left.

"Lady Sybil, may I get luncheon for you?" Pennyworth bowed toward the lass with what he must have assumed was London ballroom grace. A well brought up Sybil very politely did not laugh, although Liam found it hard not to roll his eyes at the man's demeanor.

"Yes, thank you Mr. Pennyworth. That would be very nice of you."

Miss Crawford looked expectantly at Liam, wide smile and bright eyes. He swallowed his sigh and said, "Mayhap ye would like me to fetch yer luncheon, lass?"

"Oh, aye. That would be wonderful!" She glanced around, making sure everyone noticed.

Liam rose and joined several other gentlemen at the food tables. He placed a few items on two plates and returned to his seat. Miss Crawford looked at the scant offering and took a deep breath. "I dinna think I can eat all of this, but I shall give it a try."

There wasn't enough on the dish to satisfy a small bird, but he'd guessed correctly that Miss Crawford was of the wee appetite ilk. On the other hand, Mr. Pennyworth had brought an array of foods to Sybil who was happily sampling them all. Liam dug into his food as well, all the time nodding at Miss Crawford's constant babbling.

Odd that the Scottish lass behaved more like he'd expected Sybil to act.

After everyone had completed their repast, Lady Boswick clapped her hands to gain the guests' attention. "Please form partners—one gentleman and one lady. Once we are finished with luncheon, the gentlemen will select a paper with items written on it from the pile in front of me. Ye and yer lady partner must find the items and return here. The first couple to return wins."

Giggling and shouting commenced as partnerships were formed. "Lady Sybil, mayhap you would consent to be my partner?" Pennyworth wiped the sweat from his brow as he asked this crucial question, his eyes pleading. Liam shook his head in disgust as Sybil agreed.

"Laird, I ken we will win because you are so verra clever." Liam inwardly groaned as Miss Crawford batted her eyelashes at him.

The gentlemen retrieved their list of articles to be found, and with the ladies in tow, left the area to begin their search.

Liam set off with Miss Crawford hanging onto his arm and chattering away. Did the lass ever stop to take a breath?

"Is yer home verra large, my laird?"

Ach, so now the questioning would begin. A familiar pattern he'd been through before. He looked into her upturned, expectant face and could only think how verra young the lass was.

How old was Sybil, anyway? And why did that question pop up just now? The difference between the two lasses was much more than age. "Aye. 'Tis a goodly size."

"Laird McKinnon mentioned yer lands are quite extensive, and ye two are neighbors."

He sighed. "Aye. We are."

"Mayhap I could join ye for a ride one morn to yer home? I would love to meet your mum."

He gestured to a spot in the distance. "Isn't that a bird's feather on the ground? 'Tis one of the items on our list."

"Aye!" She squealed and rushed to the feather, scooping it up. She all but skipped back and dropped it into the small bag each team had been given to collect their articles. "What else are we to find?"

"It says here ten leaves from an oak tree."

Miss Crawford spun in a circle, then stopped and pointed. "There!"

He lumbered after her, wishing the annoying game done and Miss Crawford in her nursery sound asleep. 'Twas probably the only time the lass didn't talk. He held out the bag as she pulled leaves from the tree and dropped them in. She finally took in a breath of air, and the sound of a man and woman's voices, apparently in argument, filled the blessed silence.

Sybil!

Pebbles crunched under his feet as he strode down the path and around a curve to see Sybil sitting on the ground, clutching her foot. Mr. Pennyworth leaned over her, his hands waving as he spoke.

Liam brushed Pennyworth aside and squatted in front of Sybil. "What happened, lass?"

She grimaced and shifted her body so she could look at him. "I tripped over a tree root and twisted my ankle."

"I told her to stay put, and I will go back to the castle and summon a cart to fetch her," Pennyworth said.

Sybil rolled her eyes. "I do not need a cart to fetch me. I can probably hobble my way back with the help of your arm, Mr. Pennyworth."

"Nay, my lady. You might do more damage. I shall fetch a cart."

"Oh, dear, Lady Sybil. Do you have much pain?" Miss Crawford joined the group, her eyes wide with excitement.

"I hurt my ankle is all. It is not a huge problem."

"But you should stay off your feet. Mr. Pennyworth has the right of it," she beamed at the man. "He should fetch a cart."

"Yes, that is what I told the lass. She should sit quietly while I fetch a cart."

"By the Saints!" Liam bellowed, bringing stunned silence to the group. With a disgusted look at Pennyworth, he scooped Sybil up in his arms, stood, and then jiggled her until she was settled against his chest.

"Oh, I dinna think that is wise," Pennyworth said as he stared in horror at the two of them.

"My laird, should you be carrying Lady Sybil that way?" Miss Crawford dodged his steps as he moved forward.

Liam gently nudged her out of the way with his elbow and started toward the castle. He barked over his shoulder at the two open-mouthed guests, "The two of you can finish up the game."

• • •

After a few minutes of staring up at his stony expression, Sybil said, "I can walk, you know."

He shook his head and continued on.

"Are you angry about something?"

"Nay. 'Tis sorry I am for your injury, but if I had to spend another minute in that lass's company, I might have been forced to tie my neck cloth around her mouth."

Sybil covered her lips with her four fingers and giggled. "She is very young."

"Aye. A curse to be sure."

"You were young once."

He raised his eyebrows at her. "Never that young, I can assure ye."

They reached the castle, and with the others either at the

picnic grounds or scavenging for the game, the great hall was quiet. Servants scurried about taking care of their afternoon chores. Liam stopped one of the young maids. "Is Mrs. Galbraith about?"

The maid gave a quick curtsy and said, "No, my laird. She went off to the market."

Liam nodded and headed up the stairs. Sybil twisted in his arms and looked over his shoulder at the maid. "Is my lady's maid, Bessie, nearby?"

"Nay, my lady. She went with Mrs. Galbraith."

When he gained the second floor, he headed in the direction of her bedchamber. "What are you doing?"

"Bringing ye to yer bedchamber. Then I will get a cold compress for yer foot."

"You can't come into my bedchamber!"

He grinned. "Now, lass. Ye heard the maid. No one is about to assist ye. Dinna fash yerself." He stopped in front of her door, shifting her body so he could unlatch the portal. "Here we are. I'll place ye in the chair by the fireplace and get ye something for yer foot."

It was disconcerting how the man had a habit of rescuing her and then ending up in her bedchamber. Either she'd become much more inept since she'd left England, or fate was having a grand time toying with her.

Once she was settled in the chair, he reached for her shoe, unbuttoning it, and slowly easing it off her foot. She winced as he touched the ankle. He held her foot out and turned it one way and then another, taking care to not move it roughly. "'Tis only a sprain, lass. Just sit here while I get cold water and cloths."

Sybil grabbed his arm as he rose. "See if the young maid

we just saw can tend to me." Having the young maid look after her seemed a bit less scandalous than Liam in her room, touching her bare foot, and raising her skirts to apply a cold cloth to her ankle.

She had barely recovered her breath from their walk to the castle. Her breast had been pressed up against his chest, and her nipple had tightened. The warmth from his body had heated her flesh to where she'd felt the need to fan herself. She didn't know whether to attribute her dizziness to her injury, or the scent of leather and man that wafted off him. He had carried her like she weighed nothing, reminding her again of his size and strength.

Why in heaven's name was she attracted to the most unsuitable man she'd ever met? He was a *Scot*. That was all she needed to know about him. Except he hadn't lived up to her expectations, thus far. He was clean and polite, smelled good, and she hadn't seen him swill whiskey or sneak out of a bedchamber since she'd been here. Although it appeared she found him in her bedchamber more times than she should have.

She twisted around and gazed out the window at the beautiful Scottish Highlands. Hills and valleys, mountains in the distance, everything green and verdant. He was as much a part of his environment as the trees and grass. Powerful, strong, and breathtaking, Laird MacBride *was* the Highlands.

Liam strode into the room, "No one is about, so I brought the cold water and cloth for ye foot."

No one was about and here he was in her bedchamber, again. Even with the door open, she felt vulnerable. The air snapped with the tension between the two of them, reminding her of a threatening storm. She found it hard to catch her breath as he came near and set the pan of water and cloth on the table next to her chair.

He knelt at her feet and pushed up the hem of her gown. Without meeting her eyes, he ran his hand over her ankle, then up her calf, caressing her skin, leaving goose bumps in his wake. "I need to remove yer stocking."

Unable to speak, she merely nodded. Slowly his hand crept up to her thigh where he untied her stocking, brushing his fingers over her skin, dragging the garment down. He glanced up at her as he pulled the rest of it off, his eyes darkened, his nostrils flared.

In a flash he was on his feet and striding to the door. He closed it, then turned the latch. Her heart beat so loud she was sure he could hear it across the room. Like an animal stalking its prey, Liam made his way back to her.

"Wh-What are you doing?"

He reached out and pulled her up, wrapping his arms around her waist, keeping her weight off her sore foot. "Ach, lass, you've been driving me daft for days now."

"I don't understand." Her voice was barely a whisper.

"I think ye do. Dinna try to tell me you dinna feel it, too. I have to taste ye. Feel ye warm body against my chest." Slowly he ducked his head and pressed his lips to hers. Gently, softly at first. Sybil grasped his arms, his muscles rippling under her palms as he shifted to take her in a deeper kiss.

His possession was real. He ravished her mouth, pressing his tongue against her lips until she opened. With a groan, he swept in, tasting, nibbling, sucking. Heat rose in her middle and spread upward. She moved her palms up and encircled his neck, playing with the silky strands of his hair. Her finger eased under the tie at his nape, and she yanked.

Freed from its bonds, his hair fell forward, touching her face, teasing her skin. He released her lips and scattered kisses over her eyes, nose, jaw, then to the skin under her ear. "Ach, but ye are bewitching me, lass."

If anyone was bewitched, surely it must be her. She'd never felt this way before, this need to tear off her clothes and his, so their skin could touch and press against each other. His powerful hands slid to her bottom where they caressed her, massaging, pushing her against the evidence of his desire.

"Lady Sybil, the laird sent word that you wished me to attend you?" The young maid's voice came through the locked door, pulling Sybil back to where she was. Standing in her bedchamber, behind a locked door, in the arms of a man not her husband, who had his hands where they should not be. Good heavens, what a scandal this would cause if word leaked to the rest of the party.

She pulled away from Liam, panic rising in her chest. "You must hide. I will be ruined if you are caught here."

He glanced around the room. "'Tis naught places for me to hide. Ye will have to get rid of her."

Liam helped her across the room. Patting her hair and taking a deep breath, she gestured for him to stand next to the door so he wouldn't be seen. Opening the door little more than a foot, she said, "Thank you, but I merely have a sprained ankle and the laird was good enough to bring me cold water and a cloth." She smiled, then added in a rush, "And then he left. Of course."

The maid looked concerned. "If you are sure, my lady."

Sybil nodded and began to ease the door closed. "Yes, I will be fine. My foot feels much better."

"Then mayhap I can come in and remove the water and cloths if you are through with them."

"No!" She smiled again when the woman jumped back. "I'm sorry. It is just that I planned to take a short nap, so please return later."

The maid nodded. "As you wish, my lady."

Sybil closed the door and glared at Liam. "The woman must think I am ready for Bedlam."

He strolled toward her as if they hadn't just been very close to getting caught, his eyes full of desire. "'Tis sorry I am she interrupted us."

"I am not. This could have been a disaster." She pulled herself up. "Please leave before anyone else comes."

He winked at her and opened the door, looking each direction before he turned back to her. "As you wish, my lady." With a naughty grin and a bow, he slipped out, closing the door behind him.

This wedding can't come soon enough. I must get away from that man.

Chapter Six

Sybil tapped lightly on Margaret's door. At her beck, she entered the bedchamber to chaos. It was the morning of the wedding, and Margaret was curled up into a ball on the bed weeping her eyes out. Lady Somerville stood wringing her hands while the lady's maid fluttered around with a glass of water and a cold cloth.

"My lady, thank you so much for answering my summons," Lady Somerville said.

Hurrying over to Margaret, Sybil sat on the bed and gently touched her friend on her shoulder. "Margie?"

The weeping bride rose on her elbows and wailed, "I don't want to get married."

Sybil gathered the sobbing girl into her arms. "Here now. What do you mean? You've been quite happy since we arrived."

"Duncan hates me!"

"What?" Sybil's eyes darted to Lady Somerville, who appeared ready to swoon.

"Why do you say that, dear?"

Margaret slowly rolled to her back and then scooted up so she sat against the headboard of the bed. "Um, it would be better if we could talk in private."

After years of friendship, Sybil was aware of the distance between Margaret and her mother. It wasn't that they didn't get along, but more that Lady Somerville, true to her station in life, had left the rearing of Margaret to nannies and governesses. Her parents had also spent a great deal of time in London and Bath while Margaret had remained in the country with servants. Her lonely life had led her to visits with Sybil for weeks at a time, relishing in their large, noisy, loving family.

Lady Somerville looked only too happy to leave the melodrama in the room behind. "I will be downstairs, if you need me." She quickly made her escape.

"Jane, you can leave us for a bit." Sybil smiled at the lady's maid, then turned to Margaret as the door closed. "What happened?"

Margaret took a shuddering breath. "I offered to do... you know...with Duncan last night." Her head lowered, she peeked at Sybil from under lowered lashes. "And...and..." She stopped and her face crumbled. "He turned me down!!" Fresh tears coursed down her cheeks.

Wide-eyed, Sybil sat back as her friend blubbered. She offered to do *that? And he turned her down?* She wasn't sure which shocked her more, Margaret's offer or Duncan's refusal.

After giving Margaret time to compose herself once more, Sybil reached for her hand. "What made you—um—offer?"

Margaret wiped her nose on a sodden handkerchief.

"We were kissing, and well, I thought maybe if we did *it* then, I wouldn't be so nervous today, anticipating it all."

Sybil brushed the damp curls from Margaret's forehead. "And then what happened?"

"Duncan pulled back and shook his head. I was mortified!" A new round of tears cascaded onto her lap before she was able to continue. "He said we would wait until tonight."

"Is that all he said?"

Margaret nodded.

"Why then, do you say he hates you?"

Margaret took an exasperated breath. "Everyone knows men *always* want to do *that.*" She climbed off the bed and began to pace. "He probably has a mistress that he does those things with. That is why he doesn't want me." She stopped and studied the green countryside outside the bedchamber window. "I have had to fight for my parents' notice for years. I don't want to be forced to wrestle my husband's attention from another woman for the rest of my life." She turned, red swollen eyes pleading. "Do you understand?"

This was a mess. Gentlemen did keep mistresses, and many of them even after they married. Sybil had no idea if Duncan was the type to do that, but she wouldn't be surprised if he did. Men! Why did they have to be so horrible? Her father had never dallied, and frankly, if he had, most likely her unconventional mother would have shot him. And the mistress.

That was the reason she and her sisters were holding out for love. Mother told them if a man was happy in the bedchamber he would have less reason to look anywhere else for satisfaction. As awkward as it had been to hear her mother say that, it was good advice, and so far, her brother and two older sisters had happy, fulfilling marriages.

"Margaret, dear, lie down for a bit. I will put a cold cloth over your eyes." Sybil dipped a handkerchief into the pan of water on the dresser while Margaret climbed back onto the bed. A quick glance at the clock on a small table near the bed informed her that they had only three hours until the wedding. If she didn't get her friend calmed down, dressed, and downstairs, there would be a scandal that Margaret would never recover from.

She laid the cloth on her face, and Margaret grabbed her hand. "I need to know if Duncan will keep a mistress. No matter how awful it will be, I need to know now, to protect myself." She wiped a tear leaking from under the cloth. "I cannot give my heart to a man who will break it."

Sybil patted her hand. "I will find out for you."

Margaret lifted the cloth and regarded her with wide eyes. "You will? How?"

"I don't yet know, but I promise I will find out." She rose from the bed and pulled the window curtains closed. "Just rest for a little bit. I will be back."

• • •

Liam flipped through the pages in the book resting on his lap. A small fire in the grate kept the dampness from the library. A whiskey would do just as well, but it was best to keep a clear head since he would be standing up for Duncan in a few hours. Right now, his friend was checking into a problem on his estate. Even on his wedding day, a man still needed to see to his duties.

He glanced up when there was a scratch on the door

before it opened. His heartbeat sped up at the sight of Sybil entering the room. Ach, he always had the same reaction to the lass. 'Twould be a good thing when the wedding was over and he could return to Bedlay. An attraction to an Englishwoman was not a wise thing. He rose to his feet as he greeted her. "Good morning, lass."

She had a worried look about her, darting her eyes back and forth as she moved farther into the space. "Is Duncan here?"

"Nay, he's out solving some estate matter." He set the book aside. "Ye seem to be in a bit of a dither. Is there something I can help ye with?"

"No." She started to leave the room, then turned back. "Actually, perhaps you can help me."

Liam waved to the chair next to him and sat once she settled in. He took note of her demeanor. Tension radiated from her body, apparent in the stiff way she held herself. Her whiskey-colored eyes moved back and forth as if composing her thoughts. Stray curls in the topknot securing her thick locks tumbled around her shoulders. She fussed with her hands in her lap, twisting and turning a knotted handkerchief.

"What is it, lass?" he said softly.

"Does Duncan have a mistress?" The words came out rushed and almost a whisper.

Liam reared back, his eyes wide. Saints! Did the lass just ask him if the man about to be married today had a mistress? Aside from the fact that such information was none of the lass's business, why would she even know of such things? Of course, in London everyone was debauching everyone else. 'Twas a known fact among his clan. And, he supposed, there were a few in Edinburg doing the same, but here in the Highlands, nay. A man had needs, and would take a willing wench if offered, but to maintain a woman for the sole purpose of sexual pleasure was not something neither he nor Duncan had ever done.

"Why would ye ask such a thing?"

She continued to fiddle with the handkerchief in her hands. Her heavy breaths caused her breasts to rise and fall, drawing his eyes to the delectable mounds above her bodice. God's teeth, he wanted to run his tongue over the smooth, silky skin, move his lips down and tease her nipple until it stiffened. He shifted to accommodate the swelling in his breeches. "Well?"

"Um, Lady Margaret is…um." She took in a deep breath. "She is…distraught."

He frowned, unable to understand what the woman's state of mind had to do with the lass's unusual question. "Aye."

Sybil hopped up as if nudged from behind. "She refuses to marry Duncan until she knows if he keeps a mistress."

Liam stood. "What nonsense is this? The wedding is set for today. The lass has been here for two weeks. She picks today to insist on such an answer?" He shook his head in disgust. 'Twas no surprise the bride was refusing to do her duty. Another example of the English coddling their women.

"The betrothal papers have been signed, the priest now sits in the great hall waiting for the ceremony. The castle is full to the battlements with guests. She must do her duty!"

"Do not shout at me, my laird!" Sybil drew herself up, raising her chin. "Lady Margaret is a gently bred woman who is concerned that she is about to make an unhappy marriage."

Liam waved his hand. "Marriage is not meant to be happy. It is meant to provide protection and sustenance to the woman and heirs to the man."

Sybil jerked as if slapped. "Not meant to be happy? Of course, men would think that, since they have all the freedom in a marriage. A woman must do as he says, no matter what." She leaned into him, pointing her wee finger at his chest. He fought to keep from laughing at the determined expression on her face. "No woman should be forced to marry a man she does not want to wed."

Liam opened his mouth and closed it several times, both impressed and annoyed at her railing at him. He ran his fingers through his hair. "I will send her mother to her. She will calm the lass."

"No. I have just now sent her mother away. She is no help at all." She slanted him a look. "Why will you simply not answer my question?"

He waved a dismissive hand. "'Tis naught your business."

"Then I take that as a yes." She sniffed and raised her chin.

Ach, the lass was bonny when she was mad. All fire and wrath. His lower parts tightened at the thought of all that spirit in his bed. Liam growled and grasped her by her arms. "As long as a man is happy in his bedchamber, he has naught reason to take up with another."

"That is what my mother always said." Her eyes grew wide, and her voice came out in a whisper.

His breathing grew heavy, and he pulled her a bit closer, her heady scent and softened expression wreaking havoc with his blood supply. One minute he wanted to throttle her, the next take her in his arms and kiss her senseless. From the look on her face, her feelings ran along the same lines.

“’Tis a verra smart woman, your mum.”

She nodded and licked her lips. “I’ve always thought so.” Her eyelids drooped, and she gazed at his mouth.

It was all the invitation he needed. He ducked his head and brought his lips to hers. Softly at first, until he felt her slight moan as she sagged in his arms. The warmth where their bodies joined seared him, the beat of his thumping heart drowning out all sound. He cupped the back of her neck and rubbed his thumb over her ear, his other hand on her lower back, tugging her closer to where he wanted them to join.

He shifted his head to take the kiss deeper, prodding her lips until she opened for him. With a gasp, she wrapped her arms around his waist and stepped closer, her legs nestled between his spread ones. A few flicks of his finger and the rest of the pins in her hair hit the carpet, and he fisted both his hands in her thick locks.

She was warm honey and sunshine, and smelled of flowers and woman. He devoured her mouth, slid his hands to her waist and lifted, settling her snug against his growing erection. Her increasing excitement spurred him to ease his hand around to the front of her body until he cupped her breast, amazed at the fullness, considering her wee size.

What was it about this woman that tortured him so? He flicked his thumb over her nipple, which tightened and beaded even through her gown. How he’d like to place his lips there and run his tongue over her engorged tip. To suckle her until she begged for him to take her.

He’d disliked everything English his entire life, and now he was caught in the web of an English lass. Nothing could come of this, but no matter how hard he tried, he couldn’t seem to stay away from the temptation she offered.

Slowly, he pulled away, releasing her so she slid down his aroused body. He cupped her head, his thumbs stroking her cheeks. Her eyes were glazed, her breathing erratic. If ever a lass looked as though she was ready to be carried to the nearest bed, it was the one before him. But he had to rein himself in lest they did something she would surely regret.

"I have to go back to Margaret." She stepped back, her breathing more under control.

He merely nodded, unable to utter the words he wanted to say. *Come with me to my bedchamber where I will make love to you for hours, teach you the ways of a man and a woman.*

She continued to back away, her eyes never leaving his. "She is waiting for me." Taking a deep breath, she turned and walked to the door, a bit unsteady on her feet. She opened it and stopped as he said, "Sybil."

Rounding, she gazed at him with raised brows.

"Duncan has no mistress."

Her lips trembled as she gave him a slight smile. "Thank you."

In a flash, she was through the door, the latch snapping in the silence of the room. Liam walked to the fireplace and leaned his forearm against the mantel, staring at the dying flames.

Chapter Seven

Sybil moved next to a very composed Margaret as they joined Duncan and Liam in front of the priest. Amazingly enough, despite the chaos of the morning, the wedding was taking place on time. After hearing the news that Duncan did not have a mistress, Margaret had risen calmly from her bed and proceeded to prepare for her wedding. Until she'd glanced in the mirror. Hysteria in her voice, she had proclaimed that with her blotchy skin and swollen eyes she would be the ugliest bride ever.

After numerous pans of cold water and many soft cloths, Sybil had been able to reduce the blotchiness and swelling enough to suit Margaret. The rest of the preparations had gone smoothly, and finally the bride was ready, dressed in a pale blue silk gown with a wreath of tiny Scottish bluebells in her hair.

Her first glimpse of Liam when she and Margaret arrived at the great hall took her breath away. Both men were dressed in traditional Scottish garb; kilts of their clans, with white lawn shirts, doublets, and sporrans. By Liam's side hung a sword that she could imagine him swinging on a battlefield. His reddish golden hair was pulled back into a queue and tied with a ribbon.

With their broad shoulders and height, the men seemed to take all the air out of the room, despite them being in the great hall. Sybil certainly felt as though there was a shortage of air. Her lungs couldn't seem to get enough of it. Her heart pounded to the extent she was afraid she would embarrass herself by swooning—something she'd never done in her life.

No matter how many times she forced herself to look at the priest, she found her eyes drifting toward Liam. A finer man had never existed. His strong chin, chiseled features, and full lips made small little butterflies in her stomach dance a cotillion. She snapped her head back to face the priest when Liam caught her staring and gave her a broad wink. Honestly, the man had no refinement.

I was the one staring at him.

Her flustered state kept her from concentrating on the ceremony, and she was therefore, surprised when Duncan turned to Margaret and gave her a chaste kiss before they turned to face the guests. A loud cheer went up from the crowd, foot stomping and whistles reverberating around the room. The bride and groom and she and Liam, as witnesses, signed the marriage book.

Duncan led Margaret to the head table. Liam extended his arm to Sybil, and she had a flash of being in his arms a few hours ago. Thinking of how she once again had enjoyed their kiss, heat rose from her middle to swamp her face, surely turning it red. "Are ye all right, lass?" His deep voice, lowered so only she could hear, increased her discomfort.

"Yes, I'm fine," she snapped.

He grinned that wicked smile, turning her insides to mush. "It seems to me ye are a bit disturbed."

"Nonsense, I'm merely emotional over my friend's wedding."

Liam escorted her to a seat alongside Margaret and brushed his mouth near her ear. "Dinna fash yerself, lass. 'Twas only a kiss."

He straightened and took his seat next to her.

'Twas only a kiss?

No doubt to a randy Scot that incident was *merely* a kiss. Most likely something he used with charming regularity to gain access to women's beds. Well, she would not be one of his women. She was a respectable English miss, who would never dally with a Scot.

I already have.

How did one turn off the voice in one's head that scolded and told the truth when one wanted to lie to oneself? Lord, she sounded like a nervous spinster. Next she would be searching under the bed for strange men. Or one man who always seemed to turn up in her bedchamber.

Stop it!

"I thought kilts had been outlawed many years ago?" Perhaps some conversation would restore her equanimity.

Liam turned his eyes on her, dancing with mirth. "'Twas outlawed right after Culloden, but was made legal again in 1782. Right now, the Highland Society of London is collecting tartans and identifying them with clans."

"So this plaid is your clan's colors?" She gestured to his kilt.

"Aye. 'Tis a pleasure to wear it." He took a sip of wine and studied her. "'Twas a terrible thing yer English did to the Scots."

"In war there are always winners and losers."

"Ach, so harsh ye are, lass." His eyes flashed with irritation.

She was rather glad she'd annoyed him. It seemed the only way to keep her distance from this man whose very presence disturbed her, was to provoke him. She didn't want to feel the flutters in her stomach, or the speeding up of her heart. Perhaps she was an untried miss, but she'd had enough conversations with her married sisters to know what those feelings meant. And she didn't want to have them for a Scot.

The priest called the group to attention, then offered a prayer of thanks as the servants brought out an abundance of food. Liam stood and raised his glass in Duncan and Margaret's direction. "*Slàinte mhath.*" Good health.

The crowd joined in the good wishes as platters of roasted meats, mounds of vegetables, and fresh bread and cheese were placed on the tables. To Sybil's relief, someone on Liam's other side caught his attention, and she took a deep breath. The warmth of his body continued to heat her, making her wish she had a fan like she generally carried in London ballrooms.

"I feel so much better," Margaret whispered.

Sybil patted her friend's hand. "I am so glad. You will be very happy with Duncan, I am sure. Just the way he looks at you tells me he cares for you."

"Do you think so?" Her face flushed, giving her the glow of a happy bride. Sybil was quite relieved. After the way the day had started, she would never have thought to hear those words uttered. Had Margaret truly been worried about Duncan having a mistress, or had it merely been a case of bridal nerves? Perhaps they would never know.

The whole episode made her wonder what she would do were she to find her husband had taken a mistress. Since she intended to not marry unless she found her true love, it didn't seem like something she would need to concern herself with. But if it would ever happen, somehow she didn't think she would be as accepting as other wives of the *ton* were. Nor would she seek her own lover. More likely she would track the harlot down and rip her hair out. She grinned at the picture that presented.

"What has ye so happy, lass?" Liam turned his attention back to her.

"I was just thinking how I would handle my husband taking a mistress."

"By the saints! Are ye back to that again?" He took another sip of wine, studying her over the rim of his glass. "And how would ye handle that?"

"Surely you don't want to know? After all, I have been told it is not something a young miss should concern herself with." She smirked. "Is that not right, my laird?"

He threw back his head and laughed, drawing attention from the people sitting at the table. "But now that ye have my curiosity piqued, I'd like to know what a fine English lady would do in such a circumstance."

"I cannot tell you what a fine English lady would do. Only what I would do." She gave her head a flirtatious toss. Now that they were in the great hall, surrounded by more than a hundred guests, she felt safe enough to banter with the man. There would be no kissing or touching that brought disturbing feelings here.

"So yer naught a fine English lady?" He leaned in closer,

his breath warm on her ear. "Indeed a fine English lady daesna kiss the way ye do, lass."

With one sentence he wiped out her bravado, and once more the fluttering and other disturbing feelings raced through her body.

• • •

God's bones! What was he doing? After the episode in the library, he had promised himself to stay as far away from Lady Sybil as possible. Yet here he was teasing her, and in the process driving his blood supply to where it shouldn't be. But the lass was so tempting. The fragrant smell wafting over him from her hair. The sweet smile on her face, the lovely curves under her gown.

The plump lips he wanted to plunder once again.

In truth, he'd almost swallowed his tongue when the lass had entered the room with Lady Margaret earlier. All during the ceremony he couldn't help sneaking glances at her. Her rose colored gown flowed about her like a cloud. The bodice displayed the creamy tops of her plump breasts where a gold and ruby necklace lay. Her hair had been swept back from her sweet face to gather at the crown, the cascading curls interwoven with a deep rose ribbon.

The music started, the fiddlers playing a Scottish reel. Before he could stand without disgracing himself, Brian McTavish approached the table and bowed to Sybil. "My lady, would ye do me the honor of joining me in this dance?"

A jolt of jealousy so strong shot through Liam it took his breath away. What was McTavish doing drooling over the lass? She was English and had no idea how to dance a

Scottish reel.

Just as he was about to inform the man what a mistake he was making, Sybil took McTavish's hand and stood. "I am not familiar with this dance, sir, but if you have the patience, I will be more than happy to have you teach me."

"McTavish can't teach a horse how to run," Liam snapped.

Sybil and McTavish both turned to him, the lass's eyebrows almost reaching her hairline. "I am a fast learner, my laird. I am sure Mr. McTavish will be able to keep me from embarrassing myself."

Liam snorted as Sybil moved around the table to join McTavish. What did he care anyway, if she wanted to dance? The lass could dance her shoes off and it made no difference to him. He would just sit here and watch McTavish make a fool of himself and be assured the man didn't get too close.

Sure enough after only a few minutes, the lass picked up the steps and was soon laughing as she wove her way through the line of dancers. McTavish's face flushed with the exertion as he kept up with her. The man was much too old to be making such an arse of himself with a young miss.

He leaned back in his chair, arms crossed over his chest, and watched the dancers. So strong was his concentration that a slap on his back almost knocked him from his chair. "What has ye looking like you'd like to kill someone?" Duncan grinned at him, darting his glance from Liam to where Sybil and McTavish joined hands and skipped down the double row of dancers.

"Just watching old man McTavish attempting to give himself a heart attack to impress the lass."

Duncan laughed. "Old man? McTavish is only nine and thirty."

"He looks a lot older," Liam grumbled.

Duncan pulled out Sybil's vacated seat and continued to grin at him as he settled in. "I thought ye had a definite dislike of the English?"

"Aye."

"Then why are ye sniffing around Lady Sybil's skirts?"

Liam snorted. "Nay. I have naught interest in the lass." He shifted in his seat waiting for a bolt of lightning to strike him for his lie.

"It appears to me that the lass is verra different from what ye thought." Duncan finally stopped his infernal grinning.

The lass in question twirled around, for a moment her eyes meeting his. Her face was flushed, wisps of her hair had fallen down, teasing her smooth, white shoulders—precisely where he wanted to place his lips. She glowed with happiness and joy, and all things female. His groin tightened, and he immediately shifted lest Duncan take notice and begin his blathering again about lusting after Sybil.

"Aye, the lass is a mite different than all other Englishwomen."

"Nay, my Margaret is another jewel. She is sweet, kind, and will make me a fine wife. Now, her mum, on the other hand…" Duncan just shook his head.

The music came to a halt, and McTavish returned Sybil to the table. Duncan rose and bowed, assisting her into her seat. "Pray pardon. I must rescue my wife from Mrs. Ainsley, who is sure to talk the lass's ear off."

"Is there something I can help ye with, McTavish?" Liam barked. The man was staring at Sybil with his tongue practically hanging out.

McTavish jerked and frowned at Liam. "Nay." After a

few seconds of uncomfortable silence, the man bowed once more and left them.

"That was rude," Sybil said.

"The man is a *cloun*."

She raised her chin, eyes flashing. "I found him to be quite pleasant." She paused and added, "unlike the present company."

He snorted.

The fiddlers started up a slow number, and Sybil turned to him. "Is that a waltz they are playing?"

"Aye. Another song by the great Robbie Burns."

She shook her head as more than a few dancers entered the dancing space. "I didn't realize Scotland approved of the waltz."

"Of course we do. Do ye think we're all barbarians?"

The only answer she gave him was a tilt of her head and raised eyebrows. *Mo chreach* the lass could rile him so easily.

"Do you waltz, my laird?"

He stood and took her hand, none too gently. "My lady. Will ye do me the honor of joining me in this dance?" He bowed low enough to impress a queen. Barbarians, indeed!

She rose, her face a delight of surprise, and something else he caught in her eyes that she quickly shuttered. "I would be delighted, my laird."

He led her to the center of the great hall and took her in his arms. 'Twas a mistake. The great longing and need he'd been pushing away all day rose to the surface, taking the verra air from his body. She was soft, warm, and smelled like a woman. His palm heated where it touched hers, despite the presence of their gloves. He'd been fooling himself for days.

No matter his dislike of the English, Lady Sybil had

gotten under his skin. The lass was the opposite of everything he'd been taught, and there was naught denying he wanted her. He stared down at her face, and when she bit her lip he lost his footing, almost crashing the two of them into another couple.

"You do indeed dance very well, my laird."

"My laird? What happened to Liam?"

"I think it is better if we keep things on a more formal basis." Despite her words, the lass's flushed face and darkening eyes denied her suggestion of a more reserved association. When she licked her plump lips, it took all his control not to drag her from the room and ravish her. Instead, he pulled her closer as they went into a turn.

Her gasp told him she felt how he did as their bodies touched. His blood hummed through his body, landing at a most unwelcomed place. If he didn't manage to divert his attention from the lass he'd never be able to leave the dance floor.

"When will you return to your home?" Sybil asked.

Only too happy to change the subject and get his mind away from where it wanted to be, he answered, "Within a day or two. My mum and our steward have been seeing to things while I've been here. But soon I must return to my duties."

"Is your estate large?"

"Aye. There is a wee village and many crofters living on my land. Things were difficult for a while after the Clearances, but my grandfaither managed to keep most of our clan together. When Da passed away, my mum took on a lot of the responsibility since I was not much more than a lad."

"That is odd. In England another man would have

stepped up to help with the estate."

"Nay. Our women take a great deal of the burdens. Through the years, there have been many women lairds."

Sybil grinned. "I like that. Women who are respected and allowed to make decisions."

He dipped his head to look into her eyes. "Naught barbarians, after all?" He made one final turn and the music ended. "Would ye care for a bit of fresh air?"

"Yes, I would like that. Perhaps we could get a drink first?"

Liam guided her over to a table set up against the wall and poured her a glass of ale. He raised the glass and said, "*Slàinte mhath.*"

Sybil took a sip of her ale and eyed him over the rim of her glass. "What does that mean? I heard you say that to Duncan and Margaret."

"Good health. 'Tis a common saying at occasions such as this."

Raising her glass, she repeated his words, garnering his surprise at how well she pronounced the term. Once they finished their drinks, he took Sybil's hand in his and led her to the front door of the castle. The cool air felt good on his face. They strolled down the pebbled path until they reached the small bridge over where the castle moat had been many years ago.

The partial moon shone brightly over the mountains, casting the area into a soft, magical glow. Hundreds of trees lining the mountain stood in darkness, like soldiers waiting for the word to attack. Sybil tilted her head back and stared at the thousands of stars above them. "It is truly a beautiful sight."

Looking down at her upturned face, he said, "Aye, a

beautiful sight." A feeling washed over him unlike anything he'd ever felt before, jolting him, twisting his insides at what it meant. He wanted this woman like no other. English or naught, he wanted her. In bed, in his home, in his life. He wanted to see her belly swollen with his bairns.

He took both of her hands in his, and she tilted her head to the side as she looked at him, raising her eyebrows in question. It took all of his courage to utter the words. Raising her hands to his mouth, he kissed her fingers gently in turn. "Marry me, lass."

Chapter Eight

Everything inside Sybil came to an abrupt halt. Taught from the nursery on how to deal with marriage proposals, all she'd learned fled in a matter of seconds. Had the moonlight and the magical Scottish evening tricked her? Had she downed the last glass of ale too quickly? Or had Laird Liam MacBride actually asked her to marry him?

He continued to kiss her fingertips as he gazed at her. Her insides melted as the piercing green eyes studied her, his facial expression bland. Marry? She shook her head as if in a dream, then pulled her hands away and stepped back. "No."

He grinned. "Ach, lass. I kenned it would be a problem convincing ye."

"Whatever made you ask me to marry you?"

He dropped her fingers and blew out a breath, resting his hands on his hips. "I want ye."

"That is all? You want me? Like you want a hearty

breakfast? A new stallion? A glass of scotch whiskey?"

"Nay, lass. Ye ken what I mean. Ye feel the attraction between us. I see it in yer eyes when I kiss ye, when I hold ye. Just now while we danced, I felt the heat from yer body, the thumping of yer heart. Ye want me, too."

She raised her chin and glared at him. "I have no idea what you mean."

Liam reached out and pulled her against his chest. "Ye lie. I can feel yer heart galloping now like a runaway mare. I can see the passion in yer eyes. 'Tis not possible to hide these things from me."

Sybil backed up, easing out of his loose hold. Crossing her arms over her middle, she turned to study the dark trees outlined against the mountain lit by moonlight. Marry? Indeed she had lied. She felt the draw between them, knew from the shocking books she'd snuck from her brother's improper collection that what she was experiencing was desire. And from what she'd learned from her sister-in-law and sisters, desire was a very important part of a happy marriage.

But Liam was a Scot! A barbarian. A whiskey swilling, bed-hopping, brawler. She snuck a glance at him. He studied her as if she were a bug under a piece of glass. Though in the two weeks she'd known Liam he'd never taken too much whiskey, had never been involved in a fight, and although she couldn't say for sure he wasn't visiting beds in the castle, it didn't seem likely.

"Yer thinking too hard, lass. 'Tis very simple. I think ye are a beautiful, intelligent, caring woman. Exactly the type of wife I seek. Ye must wed one day. Why not me?"

"I wasn't aware that you were seeking a wife." She purposely skipped over the part of her needing to one day wed. She'd been waiting since her first Season to find a man she loved and who loved her in return.

He shook his head. "A man with my responsibilities is always seeking a wife. Naught have appealed to me. Until now."

"You don't understand. I have always planned to marry for love."

Once again he pulled her into his arms. Tilting her chin up with his knuckle, he looked into her eyes. "I canna in all honesty say I love ye, lass, but I have strong feelings for ye, as I believe ye do for me." He brushed a loose strand of hair off her cheek. "And there is no doubt in my mind that we would be well-matched in the bedchamber."

Heat flooded her face at his words. He had every right to say that since she'd behaved like a wanton the few times they'd kissed. But marriage was a life-long undertaking, which is why she'd held out for love. True, she didn't love Liam. He was much too irritating. But nice at times. Tender at times. Handsome, charming, and attentive.

But still a Scot.

"I am honored by your offer, my laird, but I am afraid I must decline," she said stiffly.

Liam chuckled, then picked her up in his arms and swung her around. "Tell me, lass, how many times have ye practiced that in front of yer mirror?"

"I assure you I have no idea what you mean," she said, holding firm to his broad shoulders. "And put me down."

"Not until ye agree to marry me."

She closed her eyes, the spinning movement making her dizzy. Slowly he came to a halt and slid her down his body. He cupped her face with his large hands, stroking her cheeks with his thumbs. "Ye would do well married to me, lass. My land joins Dundas and is the sweetest spot in all the Highlands. Bedlay Castle, 'twas built by one of my ancestors, but we've managed to keep it well looked after."

Sybil pulled away. "I am English. I've spent my entire life in England." She swept her arm out to the darkness. "I would never fit in here." Not that she was seriously considering his offer. Was she? Married to a Scot, living in the Highlands? Truth be known, something about the place had gotten under her skin. Each day she appreciated the raw beauty of this corner of the world a little bit more.

Being raised with her brother and sisters in the country, she preferred life away from London. Oh, she had to return each year for the Season, which had actually grown quite tedious. Her twin, Sarah, had decided to remain in the country this year, since Sybil was attending Margaret's wedding. Sarah had planned to travel with Sybil, but had come down with an ague right before Sybil left, and her mother had insisted she stay at home.

"Come home with me. I must leave in the next day or so. My mum is there to chaperone, as well as my sisters. See for yerself."

"Why do you want to marry me? I am sure there are many young ladies here in the Highlands who would suit more than me."

"Nay. 'Tis ye I want. And not like a glass of Scotch whiskey, either." His voice deepened right before he lowered his head and claimed her lips in a possessive kiss, crushing her body to his.

• • •

'Twas right—'twas verra, verra right. Sybil's softness and curves fit against his body like they were made for each other. Slowly her wee hand crept up his chest to cup his cheek, stroking, adding to the burning in his belly and the thumping of his heart. In all the lasses he'd bedded in his life, none held the same attraction as Sybil. She was more than a tup, more than a way to see to his needs. This woman would be his wife.

But she is English.

He dismissed the voice in his head and released her lips, scattering kisses down her jaw to her neck. She moved her head aside, a slight groan coming from her sweet lips. She clung to his arms, and he pulled her closer, sensing the weakness in her legs. With his mouth, he nudged the edge of her gown, using his teeth to tug it down until he exposed her breast. Placing his lips there, he suckled through her silky shift.

A slight gasp had him hardening further. Ach, the lass was sweet! Before he could slide the rest of her bodice down, the sound of voices coming from the front door froze him. Quickly, he tugged her gown up, and pushed her behind him. "Fix yerself, darlin', it appears we're about to have company."

Rustling behind him, along with grumbling, assured him Sybil was righting herself. She stepped out from behind him as three wedding guests strolled down the path toward the bridge where they stood.

"Oh, good evening, my laird," Mrs. Clemmons, a distant relative of Duncan's, greeted them. "And you as well, Lady Sybil. I see you are enjoying the evening air. 'Twas a wee bit warm in there after all that dancing." She turned to her companions. "May I present my sisters, Mrs. Grayson and Lady Chilton."

Liam bowed and wished the women a good evening,

then added in his most dignified voice, "Lady Sybil and I were just returning, as the air has a decided nip and she was beginning to feel the chill."

"If ye wish to catch the bride and groom afore they retire, ye best hurry along. They were getting ready to depart."

Liam bowed again, and Sybil gave a slight curtsy. Head held high, Sybil took his arm and they walked demurely to the castle door as if they had been doing naught more than gazing at the moon. Only the lass's slight flush to her cheeks told the tale of their intimate encounter. Truly a lady, and more proof that she would make a fine wife for a laird.

The great hall was as noisy as when they'd left. The fiddler's instruments rested against the wall while they downed glasses of ale. Surely the amount of ale consumed by the guests contributed to the cacophony as voices grew louder and congratulations and salutes rang from the crowd.

"I would like to speak with Lady Margaret before they retire upstairs." Sybil rose on her toes to reach his ear to be heard. Her hardened nipple poked him through her gown against his chest. He rolled his eyes and held in a groan. The lass was too much of a temptation.

"I dinna see the lass." Liam used his considerable height to look over the crowd, scanning the gathering for the presence of the bride and groom. "'Tis my thought that we missed them."

Sybil's shoulders slumped. "I suppose I can speak with her tomorrow." Another guest, one who seemed to have been doing a great deal of celebrating, bumped into Sybil, throwing her against Liam. He put his arms out to catch her and swore at the man in Gaelic, who appeared oblivious to what he'd just done.

"Liam, I think I will retire." She glanced around, chewing

on her lip as she took in the crowd that had grown verra raucous while they were outside.

With the bride and groom upstairs, the celebrants would grow louder—an old Scottish tradition to insure the wedded couple would not be heard from their bedchamber.

"'Tis a good idea, lass. I'll see you to your door." Taking her by the elbow, he made his way through the revelers, using his size to create a path for them out of the great hall and to the stairwell. Once they reached the somewhat quieter area of the second floor, they made their way past the many doors that would soon hold guests who would stumble their way upstairs. Unless they fell asleep right there in the great hall—not unheard of at a Scottish wedding.

"Good night." Sybil reached for the latch on her door and was stopped by Liam's hand on her arm. "Not yet, darlin'."

"Wha—?" The word was cut off when he took her mouth in his. He cupped her head, turning her to gain better access to the sweetness of her mouth. Her heart thundered against his chest, in rhythm with his own. He pulled back, his forehead resting on hers, both of them as much out of breath as if they'd run up the stairs.

"You dinna answer me, darlin'. Will ye marry me?"

"I can't answer that." She drew back, her breathing beginning to return to normal. "I have to think about it."

He sighed. "I'm leaving the day after tomorrow. I want verra much for ye tae come with me. I want ye to meet my mum, see Bedlay Castle."

"I don't know. You have to give me time."

"Ach, there isn't much time, lass."

"Tomorrow. I'll tell you tomorrow."

He reached out and touched her gently on her soft

cheek. "I'll be waiting for yer answer, darlin'." She smiled briefly, then entered the room, the door closing quietly. He ran his fingers through his hair and continued on to his room.

Now he was faced with the unpleasant task of telling his mum he intended to marry a Sassenach.

• • •

Sybil awoke early, the pale sunlight barely illuminating her bedchamber. She rolled onto her back and stared at the canopy over the bed. Laird Liam MacBride wanted to marry her. If she said yes, she would remain in the Highlands of Scotland for the rest of her life, except for the occasional visits to her family home. Any children she birthed would be clan members, and raised in the Scottish tradition.

All of her close family members—sisters, brother, sister-in-law, mother, and nieces and nephews, would be in England. Yet none of that would matter if she loved Liam and he loved her. It was what she'd wanted and expected to have in a marriage her entire life. The one thing she'd been holding out for since her first Season.

Liam had admitted to having strong feelings for her, but not love. Was that admission enough to keep her from packing up and returning to England in another day or so, as her family expected? And what of her feelings toward him? There was no question that her initial feelings had changed. Time spent with him had disproven her bias against him because of his heritage.

The man hadn't been charming the ladies into his bed, had not gotten into one fight, and drank very little. Indeed, much less than his counterparts, who right now were probably suffering from the effects of their revelry last night.

She tossed off the blankets just as Bessie arrived to prepare her for the day. "Please get my breeches out, I feel the need for a brisk ride this morning."

"Yes, milady."

With very little in the way of preparation, Sybil was striding to the stable in less than a half hour after she rose from bed. She chatted with one of the stable boys as they prepared her horse for a ride. "The Laird just left a bit ago for a ride, too," he shared with her.

"The McKinnon?" Newlyweds were not known for rising early the day after their wedding.

"Nay, my lady. The MacBride." Devil take it, she didn't want to run into the man until she'd decided what she was going to do about his suggestion to visit his home. At this point, she had no intention of accepting his marriage proposal. With her feelings so uncertain, that would be foolhardy.

With the stable hand's assistance, she mounted her horse and took off across the meadow, giving the mare her head. The wind whipped her long braid, chilling her cheeks, and took her breath away. The freedom of the ride would clear her head, help her with the decision she needed to make, and indeed, she had promised Liam an answer this day.

But for now, all decisions that had her in knots were pushed to the back of her mind as she enjoyed the ride. She inhaled deeply of the fresh air. There was a lot to be said of the Highland air. Sweet and clean, with a hint of salt from the nearby sea.

After about ten minutes, Sybil slowed the horse to a canter, then a trot and a walk. With both rider and horse breathing heavily, she stopped and gazed out over the beautiful landscape. Deep green, almost hard for the eyes to look at. A beautiful place, Scotland. At the sound of hoof beats, she turned to see Liam coming toward her.

His hair was loose and fell around his shoulders as he reined in alongside her. Flushed cheeks and the panting of his stallion told her he'd been racing as well. Perhaps they both needed to clear their heads.

"Good morning to ye, lass. I dinna expect ye to rise so early. 'Twas a long day yesterday."

"It seems my body is ready to rise once the sun does the same." She shrugged. "Not very refined for an English lady, I'm afraid."

"Ach, darlin' ye've naught the ways of the Sassenachs. Ye would be a fine Scottish lass, a pleasing Laird's wife."

She shook her head. "I'm afraid I cannot make that decision yet. I don't feel as though I know you after only a few weeks."

"'Twould be a lie to say I agree 'tis too soon. I ken we would be verra good together. But what of my request that you come with me to Bedlay Castle?"

"My family is expecting me to return soon. They trusted Lord and Lady Somerville to see me here and back home safely. I believe Margaret's parents intend to leave for London in another day or two."

"Once I have yerr agreement, I will dispatch a messenger to yer family. I will write to yer brother, and assure him ye will be well chaperoned. And, if ye decide to return to England, which I hope ye do not, I will see ye there safely myself."

She held herself stiffly, knowing she needed to make a decision. Putting it off for another day or so would not make it easier. Lord and Lady Somerville would be leaving soon, and Liam was needed back home. She could leave with Margaret's parents as arranged, or take a chance on finding out if what she and Liam felt for each other was more than *caring deeply*.

This could be what she'd been waiting for all her life. She would never know unless she gave it time. Taking a deep breath, she turned to him. "Very well, I will visit Bedlay Castle."

When he grinned, a look of male satisfaction in his eyes, she added, "But I can stay no longer than perhaps two or three weeks. I will be needed at home. With three new grandchildren already this year, and my sister Marion ready to deliver her babe in a couple of months, my mother needs help."

"Ach, if ye accept my proposal, yer mum will have to do without yer help."

"But I haven't said yes. And I must have your word that should I decide to return home, you will not thwart me."

"Ye have my word, darlin'."

She regarded him with narrowed eyes. He had agreed too easily for the man she had grown to know. Hopefully, she had not just made a grave mistake. But she'd learned from watching her brother and sisters that the pathway to love was not necessarily a smooth ride.

Chapter Nine

Sybil took a sip of tea and steeled herself to make her announcement. She and Margaret were spending a quiet afternoon in the castle's solar. The room was bright and cheerful, making the most of the pale sunlight that shone through the tall windows. The tapestries on the walls depicted scenes from Scottish history, giving the room character.

They sat side by side on a pale blue settee, tea service on a small table in front of them. From Margaret's bright eyes and perpetual slight smile, Sybil guessed that the new bride's wedding night had been more pleasurable than not. The thought of a wedding night, and one with Liam if he had his way, brought heat to her face.

"I can't tell you how happy I am that you came with me for my wedding," Margaret said. "At the same time, I wish you could stay longer. Even though everyone has been pleasant to me, I still feel like a stranger."

"Even with Duncan?" Sybil asked with a smirk.

Margaret blushed so red Sybil thought the poor girl would burst into flames. Yes, it must have been a wonderful wedding night. But Margaret's statement gave her the opening she needed.

"About that, dear." She took another sip of tea and cleared her throat. "It appears I won't be leaving as planned."

Margaret's smile lit up her face. "You won't? Oh, Sybil I am so happy to have you staying for a while."

"Well… Not exactly staying."

Margaret brought her brows together in a frown. "I don't understand."

Taking a deep breath, Sybil plunged ahead. "I will be staying here in the Highlands, but Liam has invited me to visit with his family for a bit."

Margaret continued to stare, her cup of tea halfway to her mouth, which hung open in a very unladylike fashion. Not able to stand the tension any longer, Sybil reached out and gently closed Margaret's mouth with her index finger. "Someone told me you will catch bugs that way."

Returning the cup to the table, Margaret said, "Why would you visit Liam's home?"

Sybil chewed her lip until she thought she tasted blood. "Um, because he asked me to marry him."

"What!" Margaret's screech had probably made notifying Sybil's family, all the way in England, unnecessary, since the sound had probably reached London.

"*Shh,*" Sybil whispered, looking around frantically, waiting for Duncan to barge in to rescue his new wife.

"Why didn't you tell me?"

"I'm telling you now," she said with a wry smile. "He only asked me last night."

"And you accepted? And waited until now to tell me?" Margaret threw her arms around Sybil and hugged her. "Congratulations."

Sybil eased out of her hold. "Not quite yet."

"What do you mean?"

She stood and paced. "I haven't accepted his proposal because I'm not sure. I've only known him a short time. My family isn't nearby to offer advice." She waved her hand. "It's all very confusing."

"Do you love him?"

"Of course not." She paused. "I don't think so. I mean… not yet." She returned to her seat. "Do you love Duncan?"

Margaret got that silly smile on her face once again that had Sybil's insides heating up. "Yes, I rather think I do."

"So soon?"

"To be honest, I was halfway in love with Duncan before I arrived. Remember, he had visited my home several times."

"No more concerns about a mistress?"

She shook her head. "That has been all straightened out."

Sybil took her hand. "I am truly happy for you. I hope you have many years together, and many children."

Margaret touched her stomach and blushed. "Mayhap there is already a little one growing inside me." Then in a rush of embarrassment, she covered her face with her hands and giggled. "I cannot believe I just said that."

After giving each other hugs, Margaret pulled back. "When will you leave for Bedlay Castle?"

"Liam will leave today. I need to speak with your parents and pack, so he is sending his coach for me tomorrow."

Margaret leaned back, shaking her head slightly. "I simply don't know what to say. I also cannot believe this all happened under my nose and I never guessed."

"Yes. Well, I can assure you I am about as surprised as you are."

"Now that I think back on it, I do remember wondering if Liam was developing a *tendre* for you. But since I knew how you felt about Scots, I never occurred to me that you would welcome his attentions."

"The man is very persuasive." It was then Sybil's turn to blush, and they both giggled.

"Now I must seek out your mother and tell her I won't be joining them on their journey home. Liam has already sent a messenger to my brother so he won't be expecting me soon."

"I simply cannot permit you to visit with *that man* when your brother entrusted us with your care." Lady Somerville stood wringing her hands as she paced back and forth in front of Sybil.

Knowing Lady Somerville's temperament, Sybil had been prepared for histrionics, and she had not been disappointed.

Lady Somerville slid her handkerchief from under her sleeve and waved it under her nose. "I need my vinaigrette, where is that blasted lady's maid?"

The meek little maid came racing into the great hall where Lady Somerville's performance was taking place. She hovered over her lady while Lady Somerville rested the back of her hand on her forehead and sat. "Please open it for me. I feel so weak."

Sybil stifled a yawn and shared an amused glance with Margaret.

"I'm afraid m'wife is correct, Lady Sybil. You shouldn't be staying on here, especially traveling to a gentleman's home without your brother's consent."

"It is his estate, my lord. His mother, two sisters, and a full staff are there. There will be no impropriety, I can assure you. *Not that there hasn't been already—but no need to concern myself with that, since that will never happen again.*

"You should wait for your brother's consent before you hie over there, gel." Lord Somerville was making much more of a nuisance than she'd expected his wife to make. The argument was certainly a sound one, she could stay with Margaret until she heard from Drake.

"Papa, I'm afraid that won't work since Duncan and I will be leaving for our wedding trip the day after tomorrow. Lady Sybil can certainly stay here, but she would have no chaperones. It is actually less scandalous for her to go to Bedlay Castle."

Apparently frustrated with the entire business, the man threw his hands in the air, mumbled something unflattering about the female gender and strode from the room.

Lady Somerville's recovery was rather quick. Waving the flittering maid away, she jumped to her feet and glared after her husband. "Well, he was certainly no help."

"Mama, I think you and papa should just be on your way. Laird MacBride has already sent a messenger to London to advise His Grace that Lady Sybil will be staying with him."

"That's correct, my lady," Sybil added. "He has even extended an invitation to my brother and his wife to visit."

"Very well." She shrugged. "It sounds as though it has all been settled." She smiled brightly. "As soon as our carriage is loaded, we will be on our way, Margaret." Lady Somerville gave her daughter a hug and turned to Sybil. "I wish you the best, dear."

"Thank you."

That problem solved, Sybil returned to her bedchamber to assist Bessie with the packing. Still not certain she was doing the right thing, she swallowed her concerns and reminded herself that Liam had promised to allow her to return home if she didn't think they would suit.

But she wanted them to more than "suit." She hadn't spent her life thus far waiting for love to give up on it now. Love had to be part of the proposal, or she would indeed return home.

• • •

Liam crested the hill leading to Bedlay Castle. A warm sense of belonging flowed through him at the first glimpse of home. How he loved the place! From the time he'd been a lad he had always looked forward to dashing over the hill and seeing Bedlay rise in front of him—strong castle walls, the battlements stark against the deep blue sky.

With a grin on his face, he spurred the horse forward, seeing in his mind centuries of ancestors doing the same as they returned from battle. He gave in to the urge and let out with a wave of his sword and a Scottish battle-cry as he charged down the hill. His breathing increased as the horse's hooves beat a cadence under him.

As he neared the castle, two young women raced from the massive gates toward him. Lifting their skirts, they shouted and waved as they ran. He re-sheathed his sword, pulled the reins, and brought the horse to a sliding halt as they reached him. He jumped from Cadeym just as two young bodies threw themselves into his arms.

"We missed you!" His youngest sister, Catriona, wrapped her legs around his waist and clutched his neck.

"Catriona, that isna verra ladylike." Alanna, at fifteen, had begun to criticize her sister for things she'd done herself only the prior year.

Liam shifted Catriona in his arms and ruffled Alanna's hair. "Ach, lass, when did ye become so proper?"

"When Brian MacBride started paying her attention," Catriona said, then screeched as her sister pinched her arm.

"Enough, lasses!" Liam dropped Catriona to her feet and put his arms around the girls' shoulders as he led them forward. "'Tis a few minutes I'm home and already I'm listening to ye both squalling like a couple of bairns."

"How was the wedding?" Alanna asked.

"Verra nice. The bride looked beautiful and Duncan looked miserable."

"Ach, Liam, that's terrible," Alanna swatted him on his arm. "Is she truly a Sassenach?" She walked backwards as she spoke to him.

"Aye. That she is."

"And is she awful?"

"Nay. She's a lovely lass, kind, patient, and verra nice. And Duncan is anything but miserable."

Catriona sniffed. "I dinna think any Sassenachs were verra nice."

His sister's words once again reminded him of the battle he faced with not only his family, but his clan. And, truth be known, his own feelings as well. Dislike for the English had been bred into his bones. The Sassenachs were detested by the MacBrides, and if spoken of at all, 'twas always in a foul manner. But Sybil was worth the fight he would face. If only he was more sure of the lass's feelings.

Despite his mum insisting she couldn't attend Duncan's wedding because she was needed at home, he suspected she dinna want to see Duncan marry an English woman. He sighed and led the girls into the castle.

"Liam!" His mum bustled across the entrance hall, wiping her hands on her apron. "'Tis about time ye left the Sassenach and came home."

He kissed her ruddy cheek, the green eyes he'd inherited from her snapping with annoyance. "So did The McKinnon marry the woman?"

"Aye."

She shook her head. "'Twill be a verra sorry mon at Dundas in no time."

"I dinna think so. Lady Margaret is a pleasant lass. Duncan seems verra happy with her."

His mum snorted. "No Sassenach will make a Highland lad happy. 'Twas a sad day when The McKinnon agreed to marry that girl."

Already his muscles had begun to tighten with anger. He'd barely made it through the front door. Taking a deep breath he reminded himself he would soon be facing deep, lifelong prejudices. 'Twould be best if he kept his temper in check.

"Right now I'd like to unpack and look over the accounts." He headed upstairs, needing time to prepare himself. "I will tell ye all about the wedding at supper."

• • •

The evening meal in the dining room at Bedlay Castle was

a rowdy affair, with members of Clan MacBride happy to see their laird home. Liam's grandda had had interior walls built so the one time great hall was now divided into a large dining room, spacious drawing and morning rooms, and a library.

The tables in the dining room were filled with the clan members who worked in the castle. This was the only meal they shared with the family. 'Twas a long tradition, and one Liam had kept up after his da's death.

A few remarks were tossed out about the Sassenach The McKinnon had married, but for the most part nothing was said that raised his temper much. But listening to the comments made him realize how verra unfair they'd all been about the English.

Lady Margaret and Lady Sybil were both fine lasses, nothing like he'd been led to believe his whole life. Clan MacBride would need to put their prejudices aside because he was sending his carriage for Sybil in the morning, and they would all be nice to the lass or answer to their laird.

When the room began to empty out, Liam stood and addressed his mother and sisters. "There is a matter I want to speak with ye on." He glanced around at the few stragglers who remained, finishing their ale and telling stories. "I will be in the library." Ignoring the questioning looks on their faces, he stepped back from the table and left the room.

He poured a glass of whiskey, then set it down without drinking it. 'Twould be better to keep a clear head. His mum and sisters filed in, unusually quiet, which told him they ken what he had to say was important.

Once they were settled on the settee, he took a seat on the chair across from them. Leaning forward, he placed his forearms on his thighs. "I've invited a lass I met at The McKinnon's wedding to visit. Tomorrow I will send a carriage to Dundas to bring her here.

His mam's eyebrows rose. "A lass?" Then she broke into a huge grin. "Saints! 'Tis a wonderful day, indeed. Ye've finally decided to do yer duty by yer clan and take a wife."

His sisters both started talking at once. "Who is she? Do we know her? When is the wedding?"

He leaned back and crossed his arms. "Yer all getting ahead of yerselves. I've invited the lass to visit. To see Bedlay, meet my family and clan."

"Meet yer family and clan? Is she from the Lowlands? And why would ye be inviting the lass if ye weren't planning on marrying her?" his mum asked.

Liam stood and placed his hands behind his back. "If ye must know, I've asked the lass to marry me—"

Squeals erupted from three females who all jumped from their seats to hug him. With all the noise he couldn't hear himself think. "Ye need to quiet down and let me finish."

His mum was patting her eyes with the edge of her apron and both of his sisters bounced on the settee.

"I asked the lass to marry me, but she dinna give me an answer." Now that they had quieted down and he had their attention, he once again took his seat. "I asked her to come for a visit to meet everyone and spend some time at Bedlay. 'Tis my hope she will accept me after she spends some time here."

"Dinna keep us waiting, lad. Who is the lass?" Mum was almost as excited as his sisters.

"'Tis a lass that is a friend to Lady Margaret."

"The Sassenach?" Mam's smile faded and her eyebrows

rose. "I dinna ken Duncan's bride had any Scottish friends."

"Nay, she doesn't."

"Doesn't what? Yer talking in circles, lad."

"Lady Margaret's friend is an English woman. A fine lass that I'm sure ye will all love."

The stunned silence actually hurt his ears. His heart pounded as he waited for the reaction he kenned would surely come.

"Are ye telling me ye asked a Sassenach to marry ye?" Mam's voice was so low he barely heard her.

"Aye."

"Nay!" She jumped up and waved her finger in his face. "'Twill be no Sassenach at Bedlay. Ye will send word to the lass that ye came to yer senses and there will be no carriage bringing her here."

Liam stood his ground and shook his head. "'Tis sorry I am to disappoint ye, but I will not be changing my mind. Lady Sybil will arrive tomorrow and if she decides to have me, there will be a wedding."

"Nay! 'Twill be a scandal. The clan will never accept a Sassenach."

Liam drew himself up and faced the woman who had raised him, loved him, and took care of him all his life. "Need I remind ye, I am yer laird and make the decisions for the clan? 'Tis final." Unable to bear the look of shock on their faces, he turned and strode to the door.

He stopped with his hand on the latch and turned back to them. "And I'll be expecting ye to be pleasant to the lass when she arrives. Or ye will be answering to me."

Taking the stairs two at a time, he stomped down the corridor and entered his bedchamber. Going directly to the window, he leaned his forearm against the frame and stared out at the blackness. He'd made up his mind at Dundas. Lady Sybil was the woman for him. She was everything he'd ever wanted in a wife.

Now he had to convince her that marriage between the two of them was the right thing to do. He kenned that she was looking to marry for love. Could his feelings for the lass be love? He'd told her nay, but the more he thought about her, here in Bedlay, in this room, in his bed, carrying his bairn, the more he questioned exactly what it was he felt.

She would arrive tomorrow. Time would tell. If only he didn't have to fight his family and entire clan to find out.

Chapter Ten

Sybil gave Margaret a hug and headed to the carriage that had arrived to take her to Liam's home. Her stomach fluttered with nervous tension as the vehicle pulled away. She waved to Margaret, standing in front of the door with Duncan, his arm around her waist. It appeared her friend's marriage was off to a good start. They would leave today for their wedding trip. With Lord and Lady Somerville departing very early this morning, Sybil was truly on her own now. A frightening prospect.

Bessie slumped on the seat across from her. As a good employee, she would never voice an opinion of her lady's decisions, but her demeanor certainly told her what she thought of this visit to Bedlay. Sybil, herself, had to fight down the urge to tap on the conveyance ceiling and instruct the driver to return her to Dundas until her brother could send for her.

She drew herself up. No, she would see this through. She

had feelings for Liam, there was no denying it. If she didn't spend this time with him to see if love blossomed, she might regret it for the rest of her life. She'd come to realize in the years after her come-out that the elusive idea of love was not easily gained. All her married siblings had had to fight for it. So would she.

The scenery outside the window drew her in, truly a sight to behold. Hills of deep green rolled before them like waves on the ocean. The color was so magnificent it almost hurt her eyes to view it. The crisp, clean air invigorated her, gave her hope for the future. If love did, indeed, develop between her and Liam, this delightful scene would greet her each day. A burst of happiness replaced the anxiety.

Since the properties of MacBride and McKinnon sat side-by-side, they reached the path to the castle in less than an hour. Trying to see as much as she could as they approached without actually hanging out the window like some ill-mannered chit, she gaped at Bedlay Castle. An impressive structure to be sure. Stone walls seemed to reach to the sky, and go on forever. She leaned over a little bit and caught the battlements, imagining soldiers up there, arms at the ready to defend their home. She shook her head at her fanciful thoughts.

But the most impressive part of the castle was the immediate surroundings. High on a hill of verdant deep green grass, it sat about a half mile from a cliff that dropped into the raging sea, sunlight causing diamond-like sparkles to glisten on the water. It took her breath away.

Within minutes, the carriage slowed and came to a stop, and the door of the castle opened as Liam stepped out. Although they'd only been apart one day, she felt as though it had been much longer. Again she was taken in by his handsomeness. His red hair, golden streaks caught by the sun, flowed free of a tie, brushing his shoulders, stark against his white shirt. His muscled thighs, snug in fawn breeches, made her heart thump.

He looked every bit the Laird and Chieftain of Clan MacBride. She could almost hear the wail of bagpipes in the air, and the sounds of battle as swords clanged and men fell.

He grinned as he approached the carriage, his Hessian boots eating up the distance in no time. "Good morning, lass. 'Tis a pleasure to see you once again."

No proper Englishman would greet his guest dressed so informally. But on Liam it looked perfect. His deep green eyes appeared to eat her up. She found herself grinning merely because his happiness was contagious. "I am happy to be here. Truly."

He lifted her out of the carriage as if she weighed no more than a child. But then, next to his size, perhaps that's how he perceived her. She shook out her skirts, and her attention was taken by two young ladies approaching. One could say they were dragging their feet.

Beauties, both of them. The younger girl had beautiful auburn hair, braided and wrapped around her head. She shared Liam's green eyes, marking her as his sister. Her perky nose sported a light scattering of freckles—her tentative smile charming. The older girl seemed a bit more reserved, but viewed her with curiosity. Where her sister's hair was a deep auburn, this girl shared Liam's hair of ginger with golden highlights, also braided in her sister's style. And the inevitable green eyes.

"Lass, these two minxes are my sisters." He patted the younger one on her head. "Catriona is thirteen years." Then he touched the other girl on her head who rolled her eyes, obviously in adolescent pique. "And Alanna is fifteen years." He moved next to Sybil and took her by the elbow. "This is our guest Lady Sybil."

Sybil held out her hands to both girls. "I'm pleased to meet you." They took her hand, Catriona smiling shyly. While there wasn't unfriendliness in their demeanor, they certainly didn't seem enthusiastic in their greetings.

"Mum is surprised Liam wants to marry a Sassenach."

Taken aback by Catriona's statement, Sybil glanced at Liam whose lips had tightened. "Ach, and where have yer good manners walked off to, lass?"

Catriona ducked her head, her cheeks flaming. "Pray pardon, my lady."

"That is all right, dear. I'm sure it would be quite a shock to your mother." She looked up at Liam as he took her arm to escort her. "Where is Lady MacBride?"

The girls darted a glance at each other and something shuttered in Liam's eyes before he resumed a bland expression. "My mum will be joining us for luncheon. But now we need to get ye settled."

Some of her nervousness returned. It was exceedingly odd for the woman of the house to not welcome a guest. Perhaps her "surprise" at Liam's invitation to her was more than that. Hopefully, the woman wouldn't be outright unwelcoming.

Her first impression of the castle's interior was striking. The massive ceiling seemed to go on forever. Tapestries of deep blues, greens, and browns brought the outside splendor inside. A fire roared in the large dining room, which felt good, even though it was early summer. It seemed the Highlands never really warmed up.

"My laird, yer mum asked me to see yer guest and her

maid to her room since she is busy at the moment," a pleasant looking woman came down the corridor toward them.

"Mrs. Gilpenny, this is Lady Sybil, our guest." Liam turned to Sybil. "Mrs. Gilpenny has been our housekeeper since I was a lad. She will take good care of ye. I need to see to some estate business and will join you for luncheon."

"Thank you." Sybil felt a jolt of anxiety as she watched Liam walk away.

"Can we go with ye to yer room, my lady?" Catriona was viewing her as if she was some sort of a bug under a glass.

"Yes, of course. I would love to have you join me while I get settled." She glanced at Alanna. "Would you like to come along?"

The girl shrugged, but trailed them up the stairs.

Sybil followed the ample hips of the housekeeper to the second landing. They continued on past numerous doors until they came to the very last portal on the left hand side. Mrs. Gilpenny took a large steel ring from her waist and fumbled until she found a key that she inserted into the lock. She swung the door open, and they all stepped back.

It was a very small room, and it appeared it hadn't been cleaned in quite a while. The windows on either side of the fireplace were so full of soot nothing from the outside could be seen. There was a definite smell of a dead animal, and all five women put their fingers to their noses.

"I dinna understand," Mrs. Gilpenny said. "I'm sure Lady MacBride said to use this room for Lady Sybil. I thought she said it was ready for ye." She turned to Sybil. "I am so sorry, my lady. I will have the lasses up here right away to clean it fer ye."

"Thank you." Trying to make the best of it, she smiled at

Mrs. Gilpenny as she and the girls entered the room.

"Milady, is this your room?" Bessie stepped into the chamber and said, "Oh."

"It will be cleaned up, Bessie, and all will be fine. Have the trunks brought up, if you please, and we can get started unpacking."

"You sure you want to unpack, milady?" Bessie asked, looking around the space.

"Perhaps yer maid is correct and ye should wait 'til the lasses clean it up afore you unpack yer things," Mrs. Gilpenny said.

Catriona stepped forward. "My lady, we can go to my chamber and send for tea."

"Thank you so much. I think a cup of tea is a wonderful idea. And, please, call me Sybil." Only too happy to escape the gloomy, filthy room, she followed the two girls back down the corridor as Mrs. Gilpenny hurried down the stairs, Bessie in tow, no doubt to get the maids to cleaning the room.

• • •

"I told Lady Sybil ye would be joining us for dinner, and 'tis what ye will do." Liam faced his mother in her sitting room, as she had just advised him she would take her meal in her room.

She crossed her arms over her chest. "I will not sit down with a Sassenach."

"If I have my way, that Sassenach will be yer daughter-in-law."

"Nay. I will naught allow it!" She banged her fist on the table in front of her, causing an unlit candle to topple from its holder and land on the floor.

"'Tis no matter. Ye have no say, since I am yer laird and the decision is mine." Ach, the woman was stubborn. How would he ever convince Sybil he would make her a fine husband if his mum acted like a spoiled bairn? He'd kenned for years that she was not fond of the English, but he had no idea her dislike ran so deep.

"If ye would only get to ken the lass, ye will see for yerself that she's naught like other English lasses."

"Princesses! All of them. Sitting around on their arses, waiting for everyone to do for them. I spent time in London as a lass, working for a seamstress. They were the meanest women on God's earth. Always blathering about their clothes, and their beaus, and how much coin their families had." She shifted her glance from him, and said in a softer voice. "And they hated the Scots. Thought we were all barbarians. Treated me like..."

Liam hid his surprise at her words. This was something he'd never heard before. He'd always thought her dislike of the Sassenach was a result of the way her family had been treated during the Clearances. Her clan had been driven from their land to scratch out an existence as best they could. She'd often told them if his da hadn't married her when he had, she would have had to leave her beloved Scotland to move to America with the rest of her family.

"'Tis sorry I am for what happened to ye, mum."

She waved her hand impatiently. "'Twas a long time ago. But if yer guest came from London, she'll be whinin' and complainin' and demandin' from the day ye are foolish enough to marry her."

"Sybil is not like that. Ye must give her a chance." When she didn't answer, he added, "I'm asking ye to please set aside yer feelings and join us for dinner."

After a few moments of silence, she took a deep breath. "Aye."

"Thank ye." He moved to her and kissed the top of her head.

"Here ye are. I thought ye already headed back home." Liam grinned as he entered the sitting room between his sisters' bedchambers.

"We were having tea and a chat," Catriona said. "Sybil has been telling us all about London and the Season."

"Nay, lass. Ye should be addressing our guest as Lady Sybil."

Sybil shook her head. "No. I asked them both to call me Sybil. Lady Sybil seems much too formal."

By the look on Catriona's face, Sybil had already won over his youngest sister. She gazed at the lass with wonder, as if Sybil was a princess. Ach, he'd better get that notion out of his sister's head or his mum would be nodding her head and proving her point.

Alanna seemed a bit more reserved, but it was plain she didn't hold the animosity he'd seen in Mum.

He plopped into the sturdiest looking chair in the room and stretched out his long limbs. "Dinna be getting ideas in yer head about a Season, lass. 'Tis not the way of things at Bedlay."

"Nay. Sybil said after the first year ye grow tired of the constant round of balls and that finding someone to love is more important than all the parties."

There was that word again. Was missing the lass as much

as he had the day or so they were apart a sign that his heart was engaged? Aye. 'Twas possible. Every time he glanced in Sybil's direction to see her sitting here in his home, next to his sisters, looking like she belonged, his heart warmed with more than the lust his body had been dealing with for the past few weeks.

Pushing the thoughts to the back of his mind, he sat up, slapped his thighs and said, "'Tis almost time for dinner. And our cook, Mrs. MacDougal, daesna like to be kept waiting."

The three women stood and shook out their skirts. Liam offered his arm to Sybil and they left the room and descended the stairs.

The chattering of the clansmen came to a halt as they entered the large dining room. Dozens of pairs of eyes followed the group as they headed to the main table where Liam was pleased to see his mum already sat. He walked Sybil over to her. "Lady Sybil, this is my mum, Lady MacBride."

Sybil smiled brightly and gave a small curtsy. "My lady, it is truly a pleasure to meet you. Thank you for opening your home to me."

Mum's eyebrows rose, but she never gave a hint of a smile. "Aye. 'Twas what *my laird* wanted."

Sybil frowned, looking confused for a moment. Liam cast his mum a reproachful glance as his two sisters giggled. He helped Sybil into her seat and darted a glance at the girls. By the saints. Hopefully the meal would not turn into a brawl.

"Ye can all return to yer meal," Liam said addressing the clansmen who watched their entrance with curiosity. "Lady Sybil is my guest, and ye will all get a chance to speak with her." After that announcement to the crowd, conversation resumed, but more subdued than when they'd entered. More than a few people darted glances at Sybil, and he caught the word *Sassenach* several times.

"You have a lovely home here, my lady." Sybil shook her napkin out and placed it on her lap.

"'Tis ancient. And cold. The wind whistles through these walls, making ye feel as though yer limbs have frozen."

"Mum, ye ken we added wood to the stone walls in most of the rooms to keep out the cold." He spoke to Sybil. "As ye probably noticed when ye entered, we also divided up the great hall, making a drawing room, morning room, library, and this dining room. Makes it easier to keep it heated."

"That is very nice. I imagine a lot of these older castles could do with some modern improvements."

"Ach, ye won't be finding modern improvements here, lass." His mum stabbed a piece of meat on her plate as if the animal still needed killing. Faith, the woman was trying his patience. She might have come to the table, but she was certainly not ready to treat Sybil as a proper hostess would.

"We are slowly improving things. Dividing the rooms up and insulating the stone walls with wood was the first part. I also plan to add a separate room for bathing." Liam glared at his mum, daring her to dispute him. She shrugged her shoulders and continued to eat.

"Do ye have sisters and brothers?" Alanna asked.

"Yes, I certainly do. My brother is the Duke of Manchester—"

His mum snorted, but acted as if she hadn't.

"—and I have four sisters. My twin sister, Sarah, then there's Marion and Abigail who are both married, and my youngest sister, Mary."

"You are a twin?" Catriona looked at her as if she just

announced her plans to climb to the battlements and jump off.

"Yes, I am."

"That sounds like so much fun. Is it fun?"

Sybil frowned. "Sometimes it can be fun, sometimes it is not. I mean, I love my sister dearly, and cannot imagine not having her in my life, but there are times it is nice to be just myself, and not one of a pair."

"Saints! Two of ye?" mum mumbled, but loud enough to be heard. Maggie MacBride, seated at the nearest table, chuckled, then ducked her head when Liam sent her a piercing glance.

"Does Sarah look like ye?" Alanna wanted to know.

"Exactly," she laughed. "We are identical twins. Unless we wear different clothing or hairstyles, even my mother has a hard time telling us apart."

"Did you ever play a trick on someone?" Catriona's expression had Liam believing his youngest sister was wishing for a twin of her own.

"Um, actually, we did."

"What?"

"Well when we were about thirteen years, my sister, Sarah, was enamored of a young man and wanted very much to know how he felt about her. When she met him in the village bookstore one day, she pretended to be me so she could ask him what he thought of Sarah—er, her, actually."

"And what did he say?" Alanna seemed as curious as her sister.

"He told her Sarah was a lovely little girl and would be a fine woman one day when she grew up." Sybil grinned. "Sarah was crushed."

"Sneaky Sassenach," his mum uttered, this time low enough that, thankfully, only he heard her.

After dinner, the family and Sybil retired to the drawing room where Catriona continued to plague the lass with questions. Eventually, Sybil gave him a look that could only mean she was fatigued and ready to retire, but dinna want to be rude.

"Lass, it appears ye are a tad worn out, and I'm sure my sister's blathering hasn't helped." He stood and extended his arm. "Allow me to escort you to yer bedchamber."

The relief on her face had him feeling guilty for not suggesting it earlier. "Yes, please." She addressed Catriona, Alanna, and his mum. "Good night. This has been very pleasant."

His mum snorted and kept her head down as she worked on her sewing.

Once they arrived at her door, he spun her around so her back rested against the portal and leaned his forearms on the frame above her head. "Ach, lass, I thought I'd never get ye alone."

She gave him one of her slight smiles, her lips parting as if waiting for his kiss, wet and plump, and his for the taking. He cupped her cheeks and brought his mouth to hers. His kiss was slow and thoughtful, exploring the nectar of her lips. When she gave a slight moan and slid her hands around his waist to stroke the muscles of his back he lost the control he'd been hanging onto for two days.

He nudged her lips open and swept in like a wave on the ocean. He explored the soft, sensitive parts of her mouth, the taste of her spurring him to smother her lips with demanding mastery. She pressed her body against his, and his cock leapt to life. He raised his mouth from hers and kissed the pulsing hollow at the base of her throat.

Sybil's breaths came in pants, her breasts heaving, the turgid nipples nudging him through her gown against his shirt. He pulled away, matching her breath for breath. "If we dinna stop now, 'twill be impossible for me to let ye go."

She looked up at him with glazed, half shuttered eyes. He groaned and took her in another possessive kiss, sliding his hands up her ribs, brushing her nipples lightly with his thumbs.

The sound of footsteps pierced the fog of desire raging through him. He pulled back and unlatched her door, easing her body through. "Good night, darlin'." He gave her a brief kiss on her forehead and closed the door.

Turning, he saw Bessie approaching, garments folded over her arm. "Is my lady retiring for the evening, laird?"

"Yes. I believe she needs your services."

"Good night."

"Tae ye as well, Bessie."

Adjusting his breeches to accommodate the swelling, he strode down the hallway to his bedchamber. 'Twould be some time before he'd get to sleep this eve.

Chapter Eleven

Sybil rolled over once again and groaned at the pain in her back. The sun was up, and cracks in the old shutters on the window allowed enough light to fill the room so that she could see the space. Someone had, indeed, come up and cleaned the room yesterday, though the smell hadn't quite left yet, so despite the cold, she'd left a window open while she'd slept.

They must have given her a mattress stuffed with straw. It was stiff, hard, and crinkled every time she moved. The thin blanket added to her muscle pain since she'd had to stay curled up all night to create warmth.

She eased her sore body up and glanced longingly at the cold fireplace. Apparently, no maid was going to arrive to start a fire. She climbed out of bed, biting her lips against the pain in her body and the cold floor on her bare feet. When she'd stayed with Margaret at Dundas, she'd never noticed the cold in the morning. Yet it was further into summer now than it had been a few weeks ago when she'd arrived.

Bessie entered the room. "Oh my goodness, my lady. Has no fire been started?"

"No. I'm beginning to have suspicions about what is going on, but for now I will keep it to myself." Liam's mum was anything but welcoming. Some of her remarks last night hadn't made it to her ears, but she had guessed, from Liam's expression, that they were not flattering. The ones she had heard had both amused and annoyed her. It was obvious the "shock" Catriona said her mother felt at Liam inviting a *Sassenach* to his home was a bit stronger than mere dismay.

"Bessie, please go to the kitchen and fix some chocolate for me. That should warm me up. And while you are there, please see about having someone lay a fire for us."

"Yes, milady."

Since the room had no armoire, Sybil's clothes remained in the trunk she'd brought with her. She dug through the trunk until she found a thick robe and wrapped herself in it. She hurried to the window and opened it wider, hoping the sun might help warm the room.

As she turned from the window, the streaming sunlight showed only a cursory cleaning had been done. The floor had been swept of animal droppings, and water had been placed in the pitcher, but barely enough to wash her hands and face. She moved to the bed and pulled up the sheet. Yes—straw.

She didn't know whether to laugh or cry. It was obvious Lady MacBride had no liking for her, most likely because she was English. Liam's sisters, while reserved at first, had soon warmed up, and she had felt comfortable with them by the end of the night. And the kiss she'd shared with Liam in front of her door should have kept her warm all night.

For now she would keep her thoughts to herself. Lady

MacBride was a schemer, but she'd picked the wrong person to cross swords with. Sybil was no English princess, and scrapping with her sisters and brother over the years had hardened her. Despite being a duke's household, their childhood had been anything but pampered.

Her mother had romped with her children, had taken them on picnics, and had organized games for them with the village urchins. Sybil had fallen from a tree, had her eye blackened, and had been thrown from her horse numerous times before she'd learned how to ride—straddling the animal and in breeches.

Yes, if Lady MacBride thought to scare her off by making things difficult, she was ready for the challenge. The more time she spent with Liam, the more she'd come to believe he might very well be the man she had been waiting for. If that proved to be the case, Lady MacBride had just met her match.

"Milady, you won't believe this!" Bessie bustled into the room, her face a mask of disapproval.

"What is it?"

"The cook informed me there was no chocolate—in a castle this size! Lady MacBride met me coming from the kitchen and said breakfast was served in the dining room, and guests were not to be coddled. Her exact words were 'if ye mistress is wanting to fill her belly, she'll need to do it like the rest of us. At the table.'"

Sybil threw her head back and laughed. Indeed, the battle had begun.

Washed as best she could and dressed in a warm frock, Sybil descended the stairs and peeked into several rooms until she found the dining room. Apparently, everyone had already broken their fast because the room was empty. No food sat on the sideboard, and no pots of coffee or tea on the table.

Just as she was pondering what to do, a young maid entered the room. "Oh, pray pardon miss. Can I help ye?"

"Yes. I was looking for breakfast here in the dining room."

The girl looked a bit startled but then said, "Yes, miss. I'll have Mrs. MacDougal do something up for ye."

Confused by the girl's reaction, she attributed it to her arriving for breakfast after everyone else. She pulled out a chair and sat, gazing around the pleasant room. Two lengthy windows brought in sunshine, making the room much warmer than her bedchamber. The walls had been covered with wainscoting and a soft wallpaper with rows of small flowers.

After a lengthy wait, the maid returned, and quickly laid items in front of Sybil, then made a quick curtsy before scurrying from the room.

Sybil looked down at burnt toast and eggs that proved to be cold to the touch. The teapot was cold as well. She shrugged and took a bite of the toast. If she was going to do battle with Liam's mother, she needed her strength.

After eating she decided to investigate some of the rooms. Maybe she would find Liam and see if she could entice him to go on a picnic or ride. What surprised her during her quest to find Liam was how quiet the castle was. Most likely the girls were at their lessons, but Dundas had always had clan members roaming about, and a lot of loud and friendly conversation. She shivered at the somberness of Bedlay.

"There you are." Sybil opened a door to find Liam sitting behind a very large desk in what appeared to be a library. He grinned when he saw her and placed the pen in his hand on a holder in front of him.

"Well, lass. I see yer finally up and about. We missed ye at breakfast."

"I'm sorry. I didn't know you all ate so early. The dining room was empty when I arrived."

"The dining room?"

"Yes. Where I went for breakfast."

"Ach, lass. I thought Mrs. MacDougal would tell yer lady's maid when she went for your chocolate this morning. We always have breakfast in the morning room. I thought ye just needed some extra rest, or I would have sent one of my sisters to fetch ye."

"Chocolate?"

"Aye. I had someone send it from the village for ye. I ken how much ye like it first thing in the morning."

Breakfast in the morning room. Chocolate in the kitchen that Cook was unaware of? Not bloody likely. Her temper rose, but she tamped it down. Getting mad and making a scene was most likely what the dreadful woman wanted. A way to show Liam that she was a princess. She bit the inside of her cheek to keep from screeching. "I will certainly tell Bessie about the chocolate so I can have it tomorrow."

Liam rose and took her by the hand and led her to a comfortable settee near the fire. "I have some duties each day, but I want to spend as much time with ye as I can. I thought mayhap a picnic today?"

Sybil brightened. "Yes. I intended to suggest that myself."

He fingered the curls that had escaped her topknot, bringing goose bumps to her skin. "While I finish up what I need to do, why don't ye go to the kitchen and ask Mrs. MacDougal to prepare a basket for us? 'Twill be a good thing for ye to get to know my people."

If she was going to ask for a basket, it would be best to stand there and watch exactly what the woman put in there. After this morning's debacle, she looked forward to meeting the cook.

"I will do that. Just direct me to the kitchen."

After following Liam's directions, she walked into a large, airy, well-lit kitchen. The aromas coming from the room had greeted her before she'd arrived. A stout red-faced woman stirred a pot over the fire, then turned when one of the young girls in the kitchen said, "Can I help ye with something, miss?"

If possible, the cook's face grew a deeper red. Her eyes darted from Sybil to the floor, all Sybil needed to know. Apparently it had not been the cook's idea to sabotage her breakfast.

"Yes. Your laird would like a picnic basket packed." She smiled sweetly at the cook. "For two."

The woman raised her chin and said, "'Twill be a pleasure to pack a basket for ye, miss. Since 'tis for the laird, I will make sure all his favorites are in there."

"Thank you." Sybil turned to leave, then stopped when the cook said, "And what can I pack for ye?"

She waved her hand. "Whatever you pack for the laird will be fine for me." She fixed her with a piercing look. "Despite what you might have been told, I am not difficult to please."

"Ach, miss, 'tis sorry I am for the mix-up at breakfast

this morn. I dinna understand how ye was given the wrong information."

"Indeed? That is all behind us now. But since I am quite hungry, perhaps you can put a little extra food in the basket?" She winked and gave the cook a bright smile which the woman responded to with one of her own.

"Aye, miss. I'll make sure yer well fed."

Feeling as though she'd trumped Lady MacBride and turned a potential enemy into, if not a friend, at least an ally, mayhap she wouldn't starve during her visit. The thought brought her up short. She wasn't here merely for a visit, but to decide if she wanted to accept Liam's proposal. She'd been so busy since she'd arrived trying to survive sleeping and eating that she'd lost sight of her task. Did she want to be wife to Laird Liam MacBride? Was he the true love she'd been waiting for? The familiar flutters started up in her stomach once again when she thought of him.

• • •

Despite the cool air, the sun warmed them as Liam led the way on Cadeym through the wooded area to his favorite picnic spot. Sybil rode behind him on the narrow path, once again in her breeches. 'Twas too bad his mum hadn't seen them leave. The sight of the lass might have helped to convince her that Sybil was naught an English princess.

Since they'd naught been able to ride side-by-side for most of the journey, the trip had been quiet, giving him a chance to think about how he intended to win his lady over. And win her over he would.

The sky brightened as they left the heavy woods and

entered a clearing. A green meadow bursting with small flowers greeted them, with a brook running through it. Scots pine, silver birch, and heather grew in abundance alongside the brook. The entire area offered a sense of magic. One expected to see wood sprites dashing about.

"Oh, Liam, this is beautiful," Sybil said, drawing her horse next to his.

"Aye. One of my favorite spots. Many times after my da died and I was confused and frightened about leading the clan, I would come here just to think." He turned to her. "I've never brought anyone else here."

She inhaled deeply and looked her fill of the splendor he'd always loved. "Thank you for sharing it with me. There aren't words to describe how lovely this spot is."

He swung his leg over the horse and jumped down. His feet hitting the ground crushed some of the flowers, releasing their fragrance into the air. Reaching up, he wrapped his hands around Sybil's waist and lifted her. She rested her hands on his shoulders, staring into his eyes as he lowered her. Before he even let her feet touch the ground, he had taken her lips in a searing kiss.

Ach, he wanted the lass. He'd bedded enough wenches in his day, but never had he wanted one this way. Besides the throbbing between his legs when she was near, he also wanted to hold her through the night, wake up alongside her for the rest of his life. His heart burst at the thought of seeing her wee body swollen with his bairn.

He pulled away, loving the flush to her cheeks and her glassy eyes. The lass was as affected by his kiss as he was. "We had better unpack our luncheon before that growl in your stomach gets worse."

She tilted her lips in a slight smile, lips swollen from his kiss. He unbuckled the basket holding their food, then handed her a blanket. He gripped her hand, and they strolled the area, looking for the perfect place to stop. Crushed flowers under their feet gave the area a dizzying, fragrant aroma.

“Let’s go by the brook. I have an urge to wade in the cool water.”

“Ach, lass. You’ll find it more than cool. Even in summer the waters here in the Highlands never warm up.”

“You know, when we were children my mother often took all six of us on picnics. The girls would tie up their skirts and splash in the water. Many times my mother would join us.” She laughed as they spread the blanket and took the food out of the basket. “For a duchess, my mother was quite, um, shall we say, different?”

“I thought all duchesses were proper ladies who spent all their time taking tea and planning for the next ball.”

Sybil slipped her shoes off, then rolled up the bottom of her breeches, causing his mouth to dry up as he watched her slim calves emerge. He tightened his fists to keep from reaching out to run his palms over the smooth skin.

Apparently oblivious to what her actions were doing to his blood flow, she continued, “No, not my mother. She played with us, read to us, taught the girls how to sew.” She stopped her movements, one stocking dangling from her fingers. “Mother was the daughter of a third son, so her life as a child was not one of luxury. When her father died, he left his wife and only child in terrible straights. She told us if she and Papa had not married, despite his family’s objections, she would have spent her whole life as a companion to a string of irascible old ladies."

She swung the stocking to and fro as she spoke, leaving him unable to follow the conversation. Dry mouthed, he nodded and unwrapped cold meats, cheese, fresh bread and a jar of ale. Sybil drew her legs up, resting her chin on her knees. He held out a piece of bread to her, which she took and chewed. "What was your childhood like?"

Liam swallowed a sip of ale. "I was sixteen years when Alanna was born, so I had my mum and da's full attention for years. I think the only people who were more surprised than me when she, and then Catriona, were born, were my parents. Da was verra happy to have two lasses.

"But I had the usual scrapes with my cousins. We got into enough trouble to turn my da's hair white. There used to be many more MacBrides living at Bedlay Castle, but with times so hard, more than a few of my cousins left for America. Those that did stay live in crofters cottages and farm the land, grateful they haven't been tossed off."

"Ah, the Clearances."

"Aye. A bad time." He held out a piece of cheese that Sybil took and popped into her mouth. "'Tis the reason my mum does not favor the English."

"But it was so long ago."

"Resentment of the English runs deep."

After eating, Liam also removed his shoes and joined her in the brook. They did enough splashing that they were both soaked by the time they left the water and lay down on the soft grass to dry in the warm sun.

"My sister-in-law would love this place," Sybil said, glancing around at the bounty of florae.

"She is a flower lover?"

"Penelope is a botanist. My brother follows her around carrying her supplies when she does her work because she is a bit on the clumsy side."

"Yer brother, the duke? Ah, yes. I believe ye mentioned that."

Sybil turned to him. "I told you my family is different."

"Aye. Different."

Rolling to his side, he pulled Sybil close until her soft breasts pressed against his chest. He brushed the damp strands back from her face and stared into her eyes. "Ye are so beautiful, lass, ye take my breath away."

Her lips parted, and he covered her mouth with his. His hand slid down, cupping her bottom, massaging the tight muscles, pushing her lower parts against his. Sybil sighed softly into his mouth, and he swept his tongue in, tasting the honey nectar, sucking gently.

The breeches she wore had been driving him *baurmie* all morning, wreaking havoc with his senses. He eased his hand up and cupped her breast, drawing a slight moan. The lass kissed with enthusiasm, but was obviously an innocent. 'Twas fine with him. He wanted to be the man to teach her all the wonders of the marriage bed. Something he hoped to do soon.

He worked the buttons on her shirt and slid his hand inside. The feel of her silky warm skin on his fingers drove him over the edge. But a voice in the back of his head reminded him he was outdoors, and when he took Sybil for the first time, it would not be where they were liable to scare the animals.

Reluctantly, he pulled back and stared at her. "Faith, lass. We need to stop before I lose all my sense and strip ye naked right here."

She blushed prettily and quickly buttoned her shirt. Rolling away from him, she hopped up and swept the grass clinging to her breeches. "You are right. What were we thinking?" Her voice sounded as though she had just run a race.

Liam gave himself time to recover from the lust that had raged through his body only moments before, then stood and helped her gather up the remains of their picnic. He truly didn't want to rush the lass, but if she didn't say yes to his proposal soon, his brain would likely wither from lack of blood.

Chapter Twelve

Dinner was a reserved affair. Lady MacBride ate quietly, merely nodding or grunting when asked a question. Eventually, the group at the head table fell silent and concentrated on their food.

Sybil used the time to dwell on her feelings for Liam and the proposal that still hung over her head. She peeked at him under her eyelashes. Goodness, the man gave her shivers. Why she'd ever thought Liam a barbarian amused her. Even in his Highland garb he'd worn for Duncan's wedding he could only be called impressive. Dressed in shiny Hessian boots, snug fawn breeches, dark blue waistcoat and jacket, and fashionably tied cravat, he could pass for any English gentleman. But his shoulder length hair, pulled back and tied with a ribbon did not meet with the current English style.

Her mind wandered back to the kisses they'd shared on the picnic earlier. Somehow, she couldn't regret the liberties she'd allowed him. It didn't seem wrong, and he certainly kissed her in a way that made it all seem very, very right. She looked up to find him slouching in his chair, his deep green eyes watching her carefully over the rim of his glass as he sipped. She shivered and somehow knew he was aware of where her thoughts were. Unbidden, a slow heat started in her stomach and moved to her face. He grinned. She wanted to kick him, but he was too far away.

The family once again retired to the library for tea and after the cups had been cleared away, Lady MacBride stood and announced to no one in particular, "I am feeling verra tired, and will retire to my chambers." With that, she turned and swept from the room.

Liam's lips tightened, and he moved to stand, the intention to go after her evident on his face. Sybil put her hand on his arm. "I think mayhap I will find a book we can both enjoy and read aloud."

There was no point in trying to make Lady MacBride like her. Liam's mother was determined to display her contempt for all things English, no matter what Sybil did or said. Unfortunately, she had to take the woman's attitude toward her into consideration when she made her decision about Liam's marriage proposal. She would need to live here for the rest of her life. Could she do that with a woman who disliked her so much?

Catriona, Alanna, Liam, and Sybil remained in the library. The two girls played a game of chess while she and Liam browsed the shelves and settled in with a book. Despite being engrossed in their game, the girls would make a comment once in a while, which told Sybil they were following her reading of Miss Austen's *Mansfield Park*. It was a very cozy domestic scene and one that Sybil knew she could grow accustomed to.

She huffed. Except for the woman upstairs.

Liam's sisters both yawned at the same time and pushed away from the chess table. Sybil was surprised to see that she'd been reading for well over an hour. Liam's eyes were closed, his fingers linked over his middle, his head leaning against the back of the chair.

The girls whispered a good night and left the library. Sybil studied Liam for a bit, then closed the book and set it on the table next to her. She rose and smoothed her skirts, then headed to the door, only to be snatched back so quickly she stumbled and fell onto Liam's lap.

"*Oomph.* You scared me. I thought you were asleep."

"Ach, lass. I canna fall asleep with the sound of yer lovely voice reading from that book." He wrapped his arms around her and sliding his hand up her back, eased her closer until he'd taken her lips in a soft kiss. His fingers stroked the skin on the back of her neck as the kiss turned into something very different. Pulling her closer, he plundered, seizing possession of her mouth like a conqueror's spoils of war.

She attempted to hold herself stiffly, trying very hard not to succumb to the fire raging through her body at his attentions. However, she was soon draped all over him like a harlot. The heat from their two bodies seared her. Reaching behind him, she undid the ribbon, allowing his hair to cascade forward. So captivated by its silkiness, she ran her fingers through it, fisting the strands as he continued the assault on her mouth.

Liam soon had the pins from her hair scattered on the floor in front of them, and the back of her gown opened. When the bodice slipped from her shoulders, she grabbed it and pulled back. "We can't do this here. I must leave."

Without a word, he stood and placed her on her feet. She stumbled and clutched the back of the chair as he strode to the door and fastened the latch. Turning, he leaned against the door, his arms crossed over his massive chest, his heavy lidded eyes watching her intently. "Are ye sure you want to leave, lass?"

Every sensible nerve in her body screamed *yes*. But her mouth suddenly dried up and her heart began to race as he shoved himself away from the door and moved toward her like a graceful animal stalking its prey. His eyes hunted her, and she could see the tension in his body as he grew closer.

He shed his jacket and waistcoat as he walked, tossing them on a chair. His eyes never leaving hers, he tugged at his cravat; it unfurled and landed on the floor. She stared at it, mesmerized.

"I can make good use of that for even more pleasure, *mo cridhe,* my love. But not yet." He reached her and tilted her chin up with his knuckle.

"I don't understand," her voice came out raspy.

"Of course ye don't, lass. 'Tis my privilege to teach ye the ways of lovemaking." He spun her around and tugged her hands away from her gown so the bodice fell to her waist. Within seconds, the entire garment slid to a puddle at her feet. Liam pulled her back to his chest and reached around to cup her breasts as he nuzzled her neck, whispering words in Gaelic she didn't understand, but still made her blood simmer.

Sybil glanced up at their reflection in the window in front of them. The firelight and oil lamps in the room highlighted their bodies, outlining Liam's hands as he eased her breasts from her stays, massaging the mounds, tweaking her nipples. The sight mesmerized her. Her hair fell in waves against her shoulders to her waist, mixing with Liam's hair as he continued his onslaught.

She moaned, and if he hadn't been holding her up, she would have slipped to the floor. The sensations were beyond anything she'd ever felt before in her life. Her heated body wanted the restrictions of the remaining clothes gone. That thought should have shamed her, but instead the idea of being naked in Liam's arms thrilled her.

Almost as if he'd read her very thoughts, he loosened her stays and removed them, leaving her in her shift, drawers, stockings, and shoes. "Ach, lass. Ye are so warm and soft. I want ye so much I find it hard to breathe." He moved his warm mouth to the sensitive skin under her ear. Instinctively, she pushed her bottom back against his hard muscled thighs. Heavens, what was happening to her? He had turned her into a strumpet.

Sybil leaned her head against his hard chest and looked up at him. Liam's eyes shuttered as his head descended and his mouth covered hers, forcing her lips apart. He swept in, tasting every part of her mouth, the pungent scent of brandy on his breath. Their tongues tangled in the dance of lovers before he wrenched his lips free. Making quick work of her shift, he tossed it over his shoulder before going down on one knee, taking her drawers with him. His hands slid up her body as he stood. "Open yer eyes, lass. Look at the beauty ye are."

She stared, fascinated at the scene reflected in the window. She stood in just her stockings and shoes, with Liam behind her, watching her in the window as well, his hands stroking, caressing, and massaging her naked skin. A fire like none she had ever felt before raged within her. The area between her legs grew heavy and moist, with a need to press that part of her body against something.

He turned her in his arms and lifted, reclaiming her lips. She automatically wrapped her legs around his waist, pushing her dampening center to his warmth. Without loosening his hold on her mouth, he strode to the fireplace where he gently settled her on the soft carpet. He stretched out alongside her, running his palm over her curves as she faced him.

As his eyes met hers, she rested her palm against his cheek. "I'm afraid."

"Ach, lass. Dinna fash yerself. I will never hurt ye."

She shook her head. "No. I know you won't hurt me. I'm afraid of what this means if we continue."

"'Tis simple, darlin', and something we both kenned would happen. I want ye for my wife. I want to bed ye every night for the rest of our lives, see yer wee body swell with my bairn."

"But I'm still not sure," she whispered. This was a serious step and the commitment she would be making by allowing it to continue needed consideration. But her thinking was muddled, all she could see was the man who made her insides melt, and all she could think about was how much she wanted to experience what came next.

An inner voice warned they weren't even in a private place. Suppose someone walked in on them? Before she could push him away, he said, "Let me convince ye." He leaned over her on his elbow and caressed her skin, watching her with half lidded eyes.

"By the saints, lass, ye are beautiful." He brushed the

silky strands of her hair away from her shoulder and took her breast in his mouth, suckling like a babe. His hand wandered down her body, over her slight belly to rest on her most private place. She inhaled sharply at how much she wanted him to continue, to caress her in that spot. As if he'd heard her unspoken plea, his fingertip eased into her body, circling her flesh, toying with the moisture that had gathered there.

"Ach, 'tis ready for me ye are," he murmured, with male satisfaction in his voice.

The need to see his skin, to run her palms over it, beckoned her. She unfastened his shirt and felt the smooth surface coated with curly hairs that she tugged on. Liam sat up and pulled his shirt over his head and flung it over his shoulders. His chest in the firelight, dusted with ginger colored hair, all golden skin and beautiful man, rivaled any statue she'd seen in the Royal Academy of Art. His rippling muscles drew her, her hands itching to stroke his warmth.

"You are beautiful as well." She brought her lips to his flat nipple and licked, grinning when he shivered. She loved provoking that reaction from such a powerful man. Once more he eased down and drew her close, turning her so they rested chest to chest. She closed her eyes at the sensation of her bare skin touching his.

The scent of musk from his soap, along with leather and Liam, drifted between them where their bodies met. As he continued his assault on her senses, she became restless, unable to stay still. Something teased her, tortured her, made her long for she knew not what.

"Liam," she whispered, pulling away from his kiss.

"What, darlin'?" His deep voice added to her disquiet.

She squirmed. "I'm not sure. I feel very strange, like I'm missing something." Her voice sounded odd to her ears, raspy.

"Ach, lass. 'Tis yer woman's pleasure yer seeking." He brushed her damp hair from her forehead. "Let me help ye along." His fingers once again found the warm wet spot between her legs. She relaxed her thighs, spreading them further, then drew in a sharp breath and jerked as he began his circling motion once again. "Just relax, *mo cridhe*, and it will come to ye." His warm breath in her ear tickled, brought shivers to her skin.

His ministrations didn't take long before her lower muscles tightened, and intense waves of pleasure washed over her. All sense of time and place fled as she arched her back and pressed the throbbing spot between her legs against his strong palm, drawing out the sensation. She must have voiced the moan she heard because Liam took her lips in a kiss, extending the feelings by sweeping his tongue into her mouth.

Her lips were dry from the rapid breaths she needed to keep air in her lungs. She felt as though she'd run several miles. But before she could recover, Liam slid his boots and breeches off and settled himself between her splayed legs. He covered her body so they lay face to face, his upper body braced on his elbows.

She touched the beard roughened skin on his face as she felt something nudge her where his fingers had just been.

"Darlin' I would rather cut off my arm than hurt ye, but this canna be helped." He shoved his hips forward and a sharp pain replaced the enjoyment of a few minutes ago. Her eyes grew wide and tears formed that Liam kissed and sipped from her eyes. "Hold still for a minute, lass, and I promise yer pain will ease, and ye will feel only pleasure."

She fisted his hair, resting her elbows on his broad shoulders as the pain began to subside, replaced with a sense of fullness that was odd, different. He began to move in her, sliding in and out. Again she felt the build-up of pressure inside her, not as intense as before, but more satisfying.

Their bodies slid against each other, slippery from sweat. Liam rested on his forearms and cupped her head, kissing her face, cheeks, eyelids, nose, mouth—anywhere his lips could reach. He nuzzled her neck and mumbled soft words to her in Gaelic.

"*Mo ghraidh*," he whispered, "'tis better than I imagined. Ye are mine now." After several minutes of thrusting, he stiffened and threw his head back, calling her name.

His large frame collapsed onto her, but he quickly rolled to the side, pulling her over his chest as he heaved. Sybil closed her eyes, her ear heeding the pounding of their hearts in rhythm.

She awoke shivering, Liam plastered all over her. His arms were wrapped tightly around her from the back, as if protecting her from the world. The fire had gone out and she was still naked. "Liam," she said, shaking him. "Wake up."

His eyes popped open, and he smiled, starting her heart beating fast again. But there was no time for this. She needed to get upstairs before they were discovered. "We must get dressed. I have no idea what time it is." Suddenly embarrassed, she sat up and drew her legs up to cover her nakedness.

Liam, apparently not having the same issue, grinned and stretched his full length, his manhood waving at her. "Lass, don't ever hide yerself from my eyes. 'Tis beautiful ye are, and I canna get my fill of ye."

She rocked back and forth, horror gripping her at the position they were in. "It is not proper what we've done. Supposed someone comes to the library for a book?"

He reached up and tucked her hair behind her ear. "I locked the door. Dinna fash yerself, darlin'."

"Liam, please, this is terrible." Tears formed in her eyes at the thought of them being caught—naked—on the library floor.

He frowned and sat up, pulling her against him. "Ach, lass. Stop this now. 'Tis not a problem. We're getting married, anyway."

Opting to clothe herself quickly, despite her embarrassment, she eased from his arms and stood, gathering her garments from next to the settee. "I haven't said yes to your proposal."

"'Tis too late, darlin'. Ye could be carrying my bairn right now." He stood and reached for his breeches, hopping as he struggled to get his foot in without falling and knocking himself out.

She groaned and collapsed on the settee. "Oh, no." She looked up at him. "What will we do?"

Pulling his shirt over his head, he moved to where she sat and knelt beside her. Taking her hands in his, he kissed her fingers and said, "'Tis simple. We will be married."

Visions of the vile glances Lady MacBride had tossed her way ever since she'd arrived rose to torment her. Sybil had been subjected to nasty comments, downright rudeness, and any number of gestures to let her know Liam's mother did not approve of her. Life with the woman would not be pleasant, but she was his mother.

Sybil had also noticed several members of the clan had been sending malicious glances her way. Apparently, his mother had begun a campaign to drive her from Bedlay Castle.

"I still need time, Liam. I'm not sure."

He cupped her cheek in a soft caress, rubbing his thumb over her skin. "What are yer doubts, lass?"

The last thing she wanted to do was complain about his mother. It would only serve to prove to him she was indeed an English princess who couldn't get along with his family and clan. She'd have to solve this problem on her own. Truth be known, she wanted to accept his offer of marriage. And not just because they'd made love, although now that she'd sampled his touch, she certainly knew that part of her life would be a full one.

She wasn't altogether sure she loved Liam, but knew in her heart it was indeed possible. Every day it seemed more likely that he could very well be the man for whom she'd been waiting.

If only he hadn't arrived in her life with a hateful mother.

Chapter Thirteen

Liam tightened the girth on Cadeym, then swung his large body up onto the horse's back. After being away for so long at Duncan's wedding, numerous issues had arisen that he had to deal with. This trip would probably take a couple of days to hear everyone's complaints and get it all sorted out. He hated leaving Sybil after what they'd shared last night, but he'd put this off as long as he could.

When he'd left her at her bedchamber door last night, he told her he would be gone for a day or so. He'd touched her cheek and asked to have her agreement to marry him when he returned. Once more he'd emphasized she could already be carrying his bairn, which only seemed to distress her.

Her response to his lovemaking had roused him even further than he'd thought possible. He'd taken many women to his bed, but none had ever affected him the way his wee lass did. She'd created a fever in him that only she could squelch. Whatever it took, he would have her for his wife.

He wanted many years together to explore her body inch by inch. To find all the places that would set her on fire.

But 'twas not only lust that stirred him about the lass. She was kind, funny, smart, and would make a gracious laird's wife. In fact, his next trip to visit the tenants he would take her along with him, introduce her to his people. He knew she would win them over, even though she was a Sassenach. That was something he kept shoved to the back of his mind. He couldn't allow years of his mother's preaching about the English to affect his chance for a marriage filled with love and happiness.

If his mum could be won over, he was sure Sybil would say yes. He frowned, remembering some of the sly remarks and looks his mum had cast at Sybil since her arrival. The woman was so sure that all English women were princesses and would sit about waiting for everything to be done for them, doing naught for themselves. Perhaps, many were indeed like that. He wouldn't know. All he knew was his Sybil was no princess and would be a fine, sturdy laird's wife.

Catriona and Alanna had accepted the lass, looking up to her almost as if she were already their older sister. Sybil would be a great influence on the girls. Sometimes his mum was so adamant about everything Scottish that the girls never got to experience anything different.

He pushed these thoughts aside as he approached the home of Malcom MacBride, who stood in front of his house. Leaning on his cudgel, his back bent over from his many years, the old man waved his stick in the air, gaining Liam's attention. He veered Cadeym to the left and headed to the MacBride home, grateful to have his thoughts interrupted. The sooner he finished with his visits and resolving the clan's various problems, the sooner he could return to Bedlay Castle and his lady.

• • •

Sybil stared at herself in the mirror over the dresser in her bedchamber. She looked no different. Yet she felt years older than she had yesterday morning. She'd made love with a man who not only wasn't her husband, but not even her betrothed. Although, should she give him the word, she would most likely be engaged, married, and back in bed before the sun went down.

Her face flushed at the memories of what they'd done the night before. How could she have behaved in such a wanton manner? She closed her eyes, visualizing how she'd looked reflected in the window. Lord, if anyone had wandered outside they would have gotten an eyeful. At the time she'd been so "distracted" it hadn't even occurred to her. She shivered, hoping since it had been late, everyone, even the staff, had been abed.

Pushing those thoughts to the back of her mind, she hurried down the stairs to the morning room for breakfast. Although it was quite possible Lady MacBride would move the meal to another room, just to cause trouble. She sighed. Somehow she needed to win the woman over. Liam had been correct. She could now be carrying his babe. She smiled. Or "bairn" as he called it. Each day she grew more content with the idea of being his wife and living in this lovely castle in the beautiful surroundings. If she wasn't already in love with the man, it was not very far down the road.

But she refused to spend the rest of her life battling his

mother.

"Good morning," she said, entering the bright room. It was apparent why the family chose this area for the morning meal, since it faced the east, allowing the sun to lighten the room. The soft hues of the green and rose wallpaper blended well with the damask furniture in similar colors.

The only acknowledgment she received from Lady MacBride was a raising of her eyebrows. Alanna and Catriona were their usual pleasant selves in greeting her. How much fun it would be to have these two as sisters. She missed her own sisters since she'd left for this visit to the Highlands.

"We are going with our governess today for a trip into Inverness. Mum said we are to visit for three days." Catriona almost jumped with glee.

"And we will have new gowns made and visit all the shops and the bookstore."

"How wonderful," Sybil said as she shook out her napkin and placed it on her lap. "I am sure it will be a lovely time."

Alana turned to her mother, busy with her food, seeming to ignore the chatter. "Mum, since Liam is away, perhaps Lady Sybil can accompany us?"

"No." The woman's abrupt answer startled them all. "'Tis not possible." Her voice softened. "I have some things I would like to show *her ladyship*." Lady MacBride attempted a smile, but as far as Sybil could see, she didn't quite make it.

Good heavens. She was to be left alone with the witch? The hairs on the back of her neck prickled. Then she chastised herself. She'd read too many of Ann Radcliffe's works. Miss Radcliffe used wonderful descriptions of landscapes and lengthy travel scenes. But it was her use of the supernatural that had made Sybil cower in her bed many a night after finishing one of the books. Now looking at Liam's mother, she could easily place her as a sorcerer.

Shortly after breakfast, Sybil found herself hugging the girls and wishing them a pleasant journey. They hurried to the coach that would take them and their tutor, Miss Dubbins, to Inverness for a holiday. Two excited faces beamed as Liam's sisters waved through the window of the coach.

Sybil headed back to the door, crossing the large marble entry hall. Before she'd taken two steps up the stairs, Lady MacBride said from behind her, "There are a few things ye need to see to before ye take yerself off for another day of lying about, *my lady*."

So here it comes. Sybil turned, and raising her chin, viewed the lady with as much dignity as she could muster. The woman was a bully, and she'd not allow her to think she could easily dismiss her. Now that she'd had a taste of what marriage to Liam could be like—at least the part they'd shared last night—she would stand her ground. Either she would win Lady MacBride over, or convince her any battle between them would not end with Sybil as the loser.

"Yes, my lady. With what can I assist you?"

"Ach, you needn't get your hackles up, miss. I only wanted to show ye things that go on in a castle such as this. Things that anyone who felt they would want to be mistress here should know."

Apparently, Liam had told his mother he wanted to marry her. That certainly explained her overt dislike of Sybil. It wasn't just because she was English, but because her son wanted to "taint" the Scottish blood with a Sassenach.

But perhaps she had misread the woman. Maybe she truly wanted her to see what life here would be like. No doubt it would be quite different from life in an English manor.

However, the sparkle in Lady MacBride's eyes told her she had something planned that would not be to Sybil's liking.

"As you wish, my lady." Sybil came back down the stairs and followed behind Liam's mother the length of the corridor to the kitchen. Smells of meat roasting and bread baking greeted them before they entered the massive room. A huge fireplace stood against one wall with several cauldrons hanging over the flames. A roast of some sort was speared onto a spit, with a child of about eleven years slowly turning it.

The cook she'd met before, when she had requested the picnic basket, was working her fingers in a mound of dough. "Good day, mistress. What brings ye to the kitchens?"

"I don't think you know Lady Sybil, Mrs. MacDougal." Lady MacBride turned to Sybil. "This is our cook, Mrs. MacDougal."

"Nay, me lady. I met the lass a few days ago," the cook said, giving Sybil a slight smile.

"Indeed?" Lady MacBride turned to Sybil. "'Tis sure I am that there are many things she can show ye so ye have an idea how the kitchen works."

Sybil tried very hard not to show her surprise. Since when did a guest need to know how the kitchen worked? And even if Lady MacBride was introducing her as a potential bride for the laird, knowledge of the kitchen operation was generally not necessary. But if the woman wanted to play games, she would be right there with her.

"How lovely. I'm sure you can show me many things about the kitchen."

"Mayhap *her ladyship* would like to help with preparing

those." Lady MacBride nodded in the direction of a pile of vegetables in the center of a large work table where two young girls sat peeling away. The startled looks on the maids' faces almost made Sybil laugh. Obviously, no other guest had been asked to work in the kitchen.

Since Lady MacBride seemed to think all English women deemed themselves royalty, she would soon disabuse her of that notion. "Yes. I would love to help peel the vegetables." She turned to a very wide-eyed Mrs. MacDougal. "Do you have an apron I may use? If not, I can go upstairs and change into my work dress."

If Liam's mother wanted to play games, she had picked the wrong woman to match swords with. Two young girls' giggles were quickly stifled when Lady MacBride glared at them.

"Yes, my lady. I do have an apron." Mrs. MacDougal seemed flustered, but managed to secure an apron and handed it to Sybil.

"Thank you." She tied the apron around her waist and regally glided to the work table and sat alongside the girls. What Lady MacBride had no way of knowing was that Sybil's mother had oftentimes sent a recalcitrant daughter to the kitchen to help Cook as a way to remind them of all the privileges their lives came with. Even her brother, the Duke, had spent many an afternoon mucking out stables for his escapades.

Sybil picked up a knife and deftly began to work on the vegetables. Lady MacBride narrowed her eyes at the three at the table, then quickly made her exit. Mrs. MacDougal fussed around, casting uneasy glances at Sybil until finally, convinced the guest would not hurl the knife in her direction, went back to her work.

Within a half hour, the vegetables had all been peeled and Sybil had learned the two girls she'd shared the chore with were sisters, their mother being one of the upstairs maids.

"My lady, me mum says the laird has taken a fancy to ye." Meg, the younger of the girls, spoke softly, glancing sideways at Cook, apparently waiting to have her ears boxed for her impertinence. Her older sister elbowed her.

Tempted to say she'd taken a fancy to him as well, letting word spread back to Lady MacBride, she was stopped before she could speak as the woman herself entered the kitchen. "Glad I am to see ye got all that work done. I have another place that needs yer attention."

Mrs. MacDougal opened her mouth to speak, but shut it firmly when Lady MacBride scowled at her. The cook went back to her work.

Sybil stood and removed the apron, holding it out to Meg. "It was a pleasure working with you and your sister."

Both girls did a quick bob. "Thank ye, my lady."

Lady MacBride gave a very unladylike snort and turned on her heel, glancing over her shoulder to make sure Sybil followed.

The next job the woman had for her could only be called spiteful. She took her into a room with furniture shrouded in dust covers. "This room has not been cleaned in a long time. However, the mistress of Bedlay Castle must see that there are always rooms ready for unexpected company." She turned to Sybil, a malicious grin on her face. "But then, I'm sure ye aren't up to taking on this task."

"Does not the castle employ maids to see to rooms needing cleaning?"

"Aye. We do. But the poor girls are all busy and this room must be made ready for Lord Templeton who is expected in two days time." She started to leave and turned back. "Unless ye feel 'tis too difficult for ye? Or maybe beneath yer dignity?"

Sybil gritted her teeth and raised her chin. "Not at all, my lady. Not at all."

Sybil whipped the scarf from her head and collapsed onto her bed. During the past two days while Liam and his sisters had been gone from Bedlay Castle, Lady MacBride had made Sybil mop, dust, garden, polish silver, wax furniture, and just about anything else the evil woman could come up with. The more outrageous the jobs she'd been assigned, the more determined Sybil had become to best her in this contest of wills.

Many of the clan members and those who worked in the house had cast sympathetic looks at her as she went about her chores, but a mere glower from the lady of the castle had sent them scurrying back to their tasks.

Lady MacBride thought her a princess? Well, she thought the lady of Bedlay Castle a consummate witch. She held up her hands, red and itchy from the lye soap she'd been given to use for her last chore. Her back ached, her feet hurt, and all she wanted was a hot bath. But the last time she'd requested one, she was told it would be her job to lug the buckets of water up herself.

Of course, the woman expected Sybil to complain, loud and lengthy, to Liam when he returned. Then she could remind her son that all English women were useless and this one was no better. Sybil groaned.

"My lady, it is simply outrageous how Lady MacBride is treating you." Bessie entered her bedchamber with towels over her arms. "I don't know why you allow her to do so."

Sybil propped herself up on her elbows. "She's trying to chase me off. I will leave when I am damn ready to." She collapsed back down again. "Or not at all."

"You should give the laird an earful when he returns." Bessie bustled around the room, pulling out a fresh gown for Sybil to change into for dinner.

"Were you able to secure me a bath?" Sybil asked from the bed. Her eyes were so heavy, all she wanted to do was sleep.

"Yes. I managed to convince one of the lads from the kitchen to bring up some water."

"Oh, thank you so much."

Bessie hurried to the door at the sound of a scratch and opened to two large men carrying in a bathtub. "We will bring up the water for ye, lass, as soon as we get this set up."

Feeling awkward, Sybil rose from the bed. "Thank you so much. I really appreciate it."

"If ye don't mind me saying so, my lady, I don't think what the mistress is doing to ye is verra nice." The younger of the two men placed his hands on his hips and glowered.

She waved a dismissal. This was her battle and although it was nice to have advocates, the last thing she wanted to do was cause dissension among the household. It would only give the witch more fodder for her campaign.

Once bathed and dried off, Sybil passed on dinner to have a tray in her room. Of course, Bessie had to battle

Cook to get the tray. It seems the kitchen staff had been given orders not to allow trays in the bedchambers any longer. Only Bessie's persuasive skills and Cook's regret at how the mistress of the house was behaving to their guest released the tray into her maid's hands.

After Bessie watched over every morsel Sybil put into her mouth did the woman allow her charge to climb into bed, where she fell sound asleep within minutes.

Chapter Fourteen

Liam glanced up from his place at the table as Sybil entered the morning room. The lass looked fatigued, and seemed surprised to see him. "Good morning, darlin'." He hopped up and pulled out the chair next to him.

Sybil covered her mouth with the back of her hand as she yawned, and sat. "When did you get home?"

"Verra late last night. Everyone was already abed."

"How did your visits go?" Once again she yawned, her eyes watering as she tried to hold it in.

Before he could answer her question or ask about her weariness, his mum swept into the room, casting a warm glance at him, and a very cold one at Sybil. He sighed inwardly. He really needed to spend some time with mum and convince her that Sybil was verra different from her view of the English.

"When did you return?" Mum took her seat and poured tea into her cup.

"Last night." He turned toward Sybil. "The visits went

well. I had a number of problems to solve for the tenants." He paused. "That reminds me, I want to introduce you to some of the clan. They're looking forward to meeting you."

"Really?" his mum said. "And why would Clan MacBride be interested in meeting the Sassenach?"

"Mum!"

Her face colored, but her chin edged up in defiance. "I dinnae understand why a *guest* should be introduced to the clan."

Sybil reached out and touched his arm, apparently not wanting to make a scene. She was right, of course. When he and his mum had the conversation about her rudeness it would best be done in private.

"Ach, lass. What happened to yer hands!" Liam ran his fingers over her skin—dry chapped, and reddened. She quickly pulled her hand back and placed them both in her lap.

Sybil glanced quickly up at his mum who calmly took a sip of her tea, although there was a slight flush to her cheeks.

"Nothing. I forgot to wear gloves when I went for walk in the cold air yesterday. I'll put more cream on my hands this afternoon."

"The air isna that cold."

"Mayhap the English can't tolerate a bit of cool air," his mum said.

He might not be the smartest of men when it came to women, but there was definitely something going on at his breakfast table.

"Will Lord Templeton be arriving today?" Sybil asked.

"Who?"

"Lord Templeton. Your guest?"

"I know of no Lord Templeton." The lass was surely acting

strange. And what was stranger still were the dark looks Sybil was hurling in his mum's direction. Definitely something odd going on. "Faith! What is the matter with the two of ye?"

"Nothing." They both mumbled in unison.

He tightened his lips in frustration. Mayhap a change of subject would ease some of the tension in the room. "Where are Catriona and Alanna? They're usually the first ones down in the morning."

"Miss Dubbins took the lasses to Inverness for a day or two. They should be back this afternoon."

Another unusual occurrence. To his knowledge, his mum had never permitted his sisters to go gallivanting about for an overnight trip with their governess. 'Twas no matter. Now that he was home, his time would be better spent trying to convince Sybil that she should marry him.

His time away had seemed to go on forever. Leaving the comfort of her arms without a promise to accept his proposal had worn on his mind the entire time he'd been gone. Even more disturbing was how awful he felt at the thought of her rejecting him and returning home. If he cared to examine the situation a little closer, he feared he'd find his heart already taken with the lass.

Liam wiped his mouth on a napkin and turned to Mum. "During my visits, many of the clan expressed an interest in meeting Duncan's bride since so many of us have ties to The McKinnon."

"Another Sassenach," his mum muttered.

"Aye, an English lass." He narrowed his eyes. "A verra fine woman. I promised to hold a ball to welcome the new laird's wife. I'm thinking two weeks would give ye enough time to do whatever it is ye women do for such things."

"I dinnae like the idea of honoring an Englishwoman."

Liam leaned forward, his muscles tightening at his mum's continued resistance to the way things were. "As yer laird, I'm telling ye to prepare for a ball to welcome the new bride."

• • •

Sybil watched with dismay the play between Liam and his mother. Goodness, the woman was stubborn. Her face flushed and her eyes snapped, but a lifetime of adhering to the laird's wishes eventually won out, and she gave a brief nod.

"As ye wish, *my laird.*" She stood abruptly, before Liam could draw her chair out, and swept from the room, closing the door a bit stronger than was necessary.

"Truth! I don't understand the woman," Liam said, wincing at the sound of the door.

Sybil understood the woman perfectly. She was a stubborn, nasty woman who cared nothing for people's feelings. But those observations were best kept to herself. Lady MacBride also represented the main reason she was dithering on Liam's offer of marriage.

During the hours she'd spent cleaning rooms—apparently *not* needed for a guest—polishing silverware, scrubbing floors, and peeling mounds of vegetables, she'd had plenty of time to think about the man sitting near her. Just his closeness caused shivers to run down her spine. His still damp hair from his bath had been pulled back and fastened with a tie, making her ache to loosen it and run her fingers through the silky strands.

Her memories of their last time together caused her to flush and her heart to speed up. She viewed his large hands as they fingered his coffee cup, remembering how they'd swept over her body, bringing her such pleasure.

"I will be talking to my mum to make sure she welcomes Lady McKinnon."

Perhaps he was trying to convince himself, because he certainly was not convincing her. "I will be happy to help with the preparations. I assisted my mother with numerous parties and balls."

"Aye, that would be wonderful." He reached out and covered her raw hand with his. She curled it into a ball to keep him from commenting again on its condition. Doubtless Lady MacBride expected her to complain to Liam about how she'd been treated while he was gone. She would not give the woman the satisfaction of reminding her son that all English women were pampered, useless creatures. It was a battle between her and the witch. If she accepted Liam's proposal—and each day it seemed more likely—that was an issue she would have to deal with herself.

"I have things that need my attention this morning, but I would like to take you into the village this afternoon and introduce you to more of my clan."

She sat mesmerized as his thumb wandered carelessly over her hand, distracting her from his words.

"Sybil?"

"Ah. Yes." She forced her gaze up to his face. That was no better. The twinkle in his eyes told her he knew where her thoughts were. Heat rose to her face. "I would like that very much."

Before she completely recovered, he cupped her neck, and pulled her close until their lips met. The fact that her breast was practically in her tea cup barely registered as his mouth covered hers and any sense of time and place fled.

She anchored her hands on his shoulders so she wouldn't fall completely into her eggs and kippers.

Within minutes and not at all certain how it had happened, she found herself on his lap, her fingers caressing his face. Liam pulled back, both of them panting heavily. "Ach, Sybil. Ye make me daft. I want to lock the door once more and have my way with ye."

Sybil scooted from his lap and returned to her seat. "No. We were fair lucky the last time, we cannot keep this up."

"Aye, lass. 'Tis too late for that. I am already up." He grinned at her, no doubt enjoying how her flushed face colored even more.

"Nevertheless, I will leave you now." She stood, straightening her gown and raising her chin. "I must see to my correspondence. What time shall I expect to accompany you on your visits this afternoon?"

"Right after luncheon." He reached out and patted her backside, raising a squeal as she hurried from the room. His laughter echoed behind her as she closed the door.

• • •

The sun broke through the thick layer of clouds that had been with them for days when she and Liam set out in his carriage to call on the villagers. She retied her bonnet securely under her chin as the wind picked up. She'd spent a great deal of time slathering her hands with cream, but still made sure they were snugly encased in gloves so Liam wouldn't comment on their state.

So there was no Lord Templeton coming for a visit that needed the room she'd been assigned to clean. While not necessarily surprised at that turn of events, she didn't know whether to condemn or applaud the woman's audacity. On the other hand, she could be tenacious herself, and at this point she was not going to let the witch win. If she decided not to accept Liam's proposal it would not be because of Lady MacBride.

While her thoughts were wandering, they'd passed a low, stone wall that surrounded the village proper. Liam took a turn into an opening and their carriage rolled onto what appeared to be a main street. Shops lined the area on each side and several women walked along the street, holding packages, some hanging onto small children. It looked no different than any village in England. In fact, her family's country home, situated in Donridge Heath, had a small village almost identical to this one.

Liam drove them into a well-sized stable and pulled up on the reins. The familiar smell of fresh hay and horses greeted her. Dust motes danced in the air from the sunlight streaming through the small window.

"My laird, 'tis a fine day to be out and about, aye?" A stout man with a lengthy red beard wiped his hands on his pants and walked up to them, tugging on the brim of his cap. "Will ye be staying for a while, then?"

"Aye, MacDermott. I'll be showing our fine village to Lady Sybil." He jumped from the carriage seat and handed off the reins to the man. In two strides he was around the vehicle and clasped her waist, lifting her down as if she weighed no more than a feather.

"And 'tis a pleasure to meet ye, Lady Sybil."

"Thank you, Mr. MacDermott, It is a pleasure to meet you as well."

The stable man turned to Liam. "An English lass, aye, Laird?"

"Aye, and a lovely one at that."

Decidedly uncomfortable with both men staring at her and grinning, she tossed her head. "Shall we take the tour, my laird?"

Liam extended his arm, and she placed her hand there, whereupon he tugged her closer and tucked her arm all the way in, clasping her hand. "Dinna want ye to fall, lass." He gave her a rakish wink.

My, how the man can heat my blood with the slightest effort. Trying to distract herself from the warmth and enticing smell of leather and starched linen radiating from his body, she focused on the lovely village.

"Oh, I thought we were going to the same village we visited from Dundas."

"Nay. This village is home to my clan," he said as his arm swept the area.

Tidy shops lined both sides of the street, again reminiscent of her village back home. As much as she'd enjoyed the Season each year in London, it was always with a sigh of relief that she had returned to the family manor in Donridge Heath. Her only source of regret had been the realization that another Season had passed without meeting her true love. She glanced sideways at the man at her side. Could it be because her true love had never attended a London Season?

"At the end of the street there is a lovely book store. Perhaps you would like to make a visit?"

"Yes. I would love that. Perhaps we can find a new book from Miss Austen to read in the evenings."

The light jingle of a bell announced their arrival. The shop was well stocked for a small village store. After also remarking on her English background, the owner struck up a lively conversation, revealing how his love of books stemmed from his father who had been a professor at Edinburg University. "Where ye attended, my laird."

Sybil cast a quick glance at Liam. "You attended Edinburg University?"

"Aye. I studied mathematics. I've a love for numbers."

Another surprise. Although she wasn't sure exactly why. Liam was obviously a very intelligent man, a far cry from her first impression of him. How unfair she'd been in her assessment of all Scotsmen. Any guilt she might have felt was quickly squelched, however, when she remembered how he'd first viewed her. They had certainly learned a lot.

The shop owner was a pleasant man, eager to share his passion for the printed word. After a while, the discourse turned to stories about people she didn't know. With Liam busy chatting, Sybil drifted away and perused the shelves, thrilled at the selection to be found in such a tiny village.

Concentrating on the bounty in front of her, she jumped when Liam spoke. "Please excuse me, lass, for neglecting ye so."

"No need to apologize. I am enjoying myself immensely." She pointed to a stack of books resting on a small table next to her. "Look at all the wonderful novels I found."

"'Twill be a pleasure to hear you read to me at night." The twinkle in his eyes said something different than his words.

Not wanting to have to fan her face again to keep the heat down, she quickly retrieved the books and headed to the counter. His soft laughter followed her down the aisle.

Loaded down with her purchases—including Miss

Austen's new book—they left the shop.

They strolled through the village, stopping to chat, and every person she met was pleasant and welcoming. It was truly too bad the one person whose regard she would like treated her like a pariah. The shops they entered were well appointed and managed by stocky, cheerful people. She was particularly taken with Mrs. Amish MacBride who sold lovely, soft Scottish woolen sweaters and scarves made by her and her five daughters.

Before she could refuse, Liam had asked Mrs. MacBride to fashion a scarf and glove set for her. The sparkle in the woman's eyes radiated approval of her laird and the lady he accompanied. Sybil felt the happiest she'd been since she'd arrived at Bedlay. Not everyone, apparently, held her in disdain.

"I would love a cup of tea." Sybil glanced up and down the street. "Is there an inn nearby?"

"Aye. A fine inn where ye can have yer tea and I can get a cool drink a bit more to my liking."

"And what scandalous name does this inn have?"

"Naught, darlin'. This one is verra nicely named The Drovers Inn."

"How interesting? Does that have a particular meaning?"

"That it does, lass. 'Tis an old coaching inn from my great grandda's time. 'Twas once used as a place to quench yer thirst by the Highland drovers who used to drive their cattle down the side of the mountains to the markets in the south."

"I am certainly getting my fill of Scottish history on this trip. There is so much I hadn't known about Scotland. It is sad your rebellious uprising was squashed, and so many were driven from the land. But, on the other hand, every war has winners and losers. With England being the great country she is, we would naturally have more wins on our side."

He cast her a strange look. "Aye. I guess that would be yer feeling as a Sassenach."

His remark stung. After what they'd shared, he still thought of her as an outlander?

The owners of the inn, another MacBride and his wife, greeted Liam as if he were a long lost son. One thing she had been impressed by all afternoon was the affection between Liam and his clansmen, and how free and easy their attitude was toward their laird. Apparently, there was nothing stiff or remote about how he handled his people.

But there had been that Sassenach comment.

• • •

Liam was pleased at how well most of his clansmen received Sybil. Although all had remarked on her English lineage, only a few appeared perturbed that a Sassenach was in the company of their laird. He was confident he could sway them to his side. Sybil was a very likeable person. So far, his mum was the only opponent to the lass. Her attitude was something he had to deal with. And verra soon.

He'd tried very hard to ignore Sybil's remark about the "great" country of England. Of course she would feel that way, having been raised with certain expectations. One of them being the idea that her country was always right. Hopefully, she wouldn't say something similar in front of his mum, giving her more reason to criticize her.

"Which of Miss Austen's books will ye be reading to us?" Liam settled on the settee in front of the fire in the library.

Once again, Catriona and Alanna faced each other over a chessboard and mum had retired right from the dining table.

A kitchen helper carried in the tea tray, and Sybil rose to pour for them all. She looked so at home here and ready to take on the role of the laird's wife. With her delicate hands—which had recovered somewhat from whatever it was that had ruined them—she poured tea and passed cups and small plates with slices of Mrs. MacDougal's cherry cake and butter tarts. After settling next to him, she picked up a copy of *Emma* and began to read.

Once again, Liam leaned his head back against the chair and allowed the melody of her voice to wash over him. Her tone rose and fell, using different voices for the characters. How he wished they were both in his massive bed upstairs—naked—as she read to him. He would entertain himself by caressing her soft skin and teasing her taut nipples until her words faltered. Then, when her skin flushed a bright red and her eyes grew dark, he would remove the book from her hand, place it on the table next to his bed, and make slow, sweet love to her.

Soon he would press her for an answer. Certainly, she knew by now that what they shared was enough to build a happy marriage on. The lass had stated she would not marry for any reason except love. It didn't take much convincing to admit he loved the lass. She was sweet, strong, loyal, and had charmed many of his clansmen. His sisters were quite fond of her, and already asked her advice as if she were an older sister.

Then, as if a cloud passed over the sun leaving him chilled, an image of mum snarling "Sassenach" at his beloved soured him. He would speak with the woman soon. Either she would come to terms with his decision or face the consequences. Hopefully, she wouldn't force his hand in the matter.

After bringing his mum around to his way of thinking, he needed to convince Sybil that her place was here with him. A locked library door, providing them with much needed privacy once the lasses left for bed, would be just the thing. He smiled in anticipation.

Chapter Fifteen

Sybil lay sprawled on the carpet in front of the fire. Naked. As much as she had promised herself she would not allow a repeat of their prior scandalous behavior in the library, here she was trying desperately to remember where she'd placed her bones, because apparently they were missing, along with her clothing.

"Lass, I would have yer answer," Liam said.

She moved her head to regard him, his large body flung out alongside her, a mellow look on his handsome face.

"What answer?"

Rolling to his side, he bent his elbow and propped his head on his hand, his deep green eyes riveted on her. "Ye know what answer I'm waiting for."

She smiled. "Oh, that one."

"Aye, that one."

How tempted she was to just throw her arms around his neck and shout "yes!" Her heart knew. Her body knew.

But her brain stopped her cold in her tracks. And with good cause. There was a definite mean streak in Lady MacBride that, thankfully, she hadn't seemed to pass onto any of her children. Liam and his two sisters were kind, thoughtful, and easy to be around. Simply put, his mother was not.

She chewed her lip as she studied him. The face she'd grown to love, the body she'd discovered brought her pleasure beyond any of her imaginings. She could easily spend the rest of her life living here, loving him, bearing his children. If only.

"I enjoyed meeting your people yesterday." She paused and chose her words carefully. "I already love your sisters. They are sweet and wonderful young ladies." Unable to continue, she looked off into the distance. How to tell a man his mother was a witch?

Liam wrapped one of her curls around his finger. "Ye are having thoughts about my mum."

Exhaling a deep breath, she said, "Yes. I think she not only disapproves of me, but actually dislikes me a great deal, and I honestly do not know why."

Releasing her hair, he rolled over onto this back and crossed his large hands over his chest. "Only because yer English. She has a dislike for the Sassenach."

"To her I'm a Sassenach, but to me she is a Scot. If I'm willing to overlook that, she should be able to do the same."

"Ach, the woman has a life-long dislike of the English." He cast her a rueful glance. "And are ye overlooking that I'm a Scot, too?"

She did not like the turn of the conversation. This could be very delicate ground they were treading. Disliking someone because of their actions was understandable. There were many frivolous members of the *ton* she disliked due to their behavior and reputation. But she'd done nothing to make Lady MacBride hate her so. To disdain an entire group of people merely because of where they'd been born made no sense whatsoever. After all, she was willing to put aside her ingrained suspicion of the Scottish, and how she'd always viewed the men.

He cupped her chin and turned her head in his direction. "Ye would be marrying me, lass. Not my mum."

So easily said, yet so difficult to live with. Difficult enough that she was very reluctant to give Liam the answer he wanted. Marriage was forever. If she couldn't win over Lady MacBride, her whole life could be one of misery. She had no trouble standing up to the woman, but was it fair to bring such strife and unhappiness to the entire household and Clan MacBride?

Sybil sat up and began to gather her clothing. "I received a letter from my mother today. She is concerned that I have imposed upon your hospitality far too long."

"And did ye tell your mum that ye are not imposing since you will be mistress of Bedlay Castle one day soon?"

"That hasn't been decided yet. She reminded me in her letter that Marion's time grows near, and she knows I want to be there for that." She dropped her shift over her head and wrestled into the arms, then picking up her stays she turned her back to Liam. "Can you lace me, please?"

He took them from her hands and started the lacing process, grumbling, "I prefer to be taking them off."

What she faced was a true conundrum. Perhaps when Margaret and her new husband came for the ball in their honor she might gain some insight and help from her friend. If nothing else, she would at least obtain a willing ear. She needed to make a decision about Liam's proposal, and whether she truly wanted a life away from England, and among Scots, for the rest of her life.

She was yanked back from her musing by Liam's deep voice as it rumbled through her. "Yer thinking too much, lass." He turned her body to face him. "There are only two people involved in yer decision.

"I ken a marriage between us would be a good thing for you, me, and my clan. That is all that matters." He kissed her gently on her forehead. "I want ye for my wife, Lady Sybil Lacey. And be warned, lass, I won't give up until I have yer consent."

• • •

Sybil waited anxiously on the steps of Bedlay Castle as the coach carrying Duncan and Margaret rolled to a stop. Liam stood alongside her, his hand on her elbow. "Relax, lass. I can feel you trembling."

She smiled brightly. "I am just so excited to see Margaret. It feels like many months since I've seen her, instead of merely one."

Duncan alighted from the carriage and turned to help his new wife. Margaret stepped down and immediately exclaimed, "Sybil!"

Unable to hold her any longer, Liam released Sybil's elbow as she hurried forward and embraced her friend. The women hugged and exclaimed over their separation. Duncan strode up to Liam and clasped his hand and gripped his shoulder. "The lasses behave as if they haven't seen each other in months."

"Aye. Sybil's been flustered all morn." He chuckled to

himself at her fussing since they'd risen from the breakfast table. Since his mum had excused herself, stating her intention to see to the last minute details of his sisters' gowns, Sybil had stepped in as hostess. She had certainly been well-trained in the art of preparing for and receiving guests. Despite her excitement at seeing her friend once more, she'd inspected the newly cleaned guest bedchamber, discussed the menus with Mrs. MacDougal, arranged flowers throughout the downstairs, and still managed to look beautiful.

"And how long do ye plan to keep the lass prisoner at Bedlay Castle?" Duncan smirked as they watched the ladies chattering like two magpies.

Liam grinned and crossed his arms over his chest. "Till she answers a question I put to her."

Duncan's brows rose. "And that would be?"

Liam hesitated, then said, "I asked Lady Sybil to marry me once again."

Duncan slapped Liam on the back. "'Tis not a surpise. Ye said as much before ye left Dundas. I believe that was the purpose of bringing her here. To meet yer family and the Clan."

"Aye. And I hoped doing just that would convince her."

"Ye don't sound as if the plan has worked."

Liam shook his head. "My mum has been outspoken about her dislike of the English. Sybil has been patient with her, but I ken that is what's holding the lass back."

"Mayhap 'tis time to talk to yer mum. No offense, but she's always been a bit sour, even with yer da."

Running his fingers through his hair, Liam nodded. "Aye. She does allow her tongue to run on too much. I've never stopped her before, but 'tis time to let her ken I'm her laird, and the choice is mine."

Arm-in-arm, Sybil and Margaret strolled to the castle door. 'Twas the happiest he'd seen her since she had arrived a month ago. She waved her hand in the air as she spoke, her cheeks flushed, her eyes sparkling. Liam's gut tightened at the sight. The time had indeed come to take his mum to task and end this war she'd created.

• • •

The ball in honor of The McKinnon and his bride turned out to be the most magical night of Sybil's life. During her four Seasons, she'd danced with numerous men in dozens of English ballrooms, but none had moved her quite the way Liam did. Not that he was a better dancer. In fact, he lacked the smoothness and polish of the better Englishmen. But when he held her close in a waltz, pulling her even nearer when they went into a turn, for the first time in her life she felt as if she would swoon.

She'd also been approached by many of the MacBride Clan to dance a Scottish reel or a quadrille. But it was always back in Liam's arms where she'd felt a rush of excitement and joy. She found herself wanting to giggle every time he glanced her way. She'd never been that type of woman and used to smirk at other girls who would have that sort of a response to a man's attention.

Yet her giggle would turn to desire when he slanted a smoldering look in her direction as he conversed with another guest. Goodness, the man could set her heart to thumping and her stomach to quivering so easily. But was that love? Or merely lust?

Now, she and Margaret sat on Sybil's bed going over the

evening and sharing stories much like they'd done for years when they were in London during the Season. Generally, her twin, Sarah, would be right there with them. It was times like this that she missed her sister the most. If she did decide to accept Liam's proposal she would insist that Sarah stay for a while after the wedding.

The wedding! Heavens had she gotten that far that she could think of her wedding? Perhaps it was time to put Liam out of his misery and accept his offer. She grinned at the thought of how they would celebrate her decision.

"What are you grinning at?" Margaret's voice broke into her reverie, reminding her she was being especially rude by ignoring her guest.

"Oh, nothing in particular."

Margaret's eyebrows rose. "Indeed? Why do I get the feeling you were thinking about a certain handsome Scot who could not keep his eyes off you all evening?"

Sybil felt the blush start at her toes and climb all the way to her face. Had Liam been that obvious? "I don't suppose there is any point in denying it."

"Not at all. Have you accepted his offer of marriage?"

Sybil sighed. "Not yet."

"It is obvious the man adores you. You should have seen his face every time you were on the dance floor with another man. When one of his clan asked you to waltz, I thought Liam would break the poor man's arm wrestling you away from him." Margaret covered her mouth and laughed. She paused and took Sybil's hand. "Why haven't you accepted his offer? Do you not feel the love for him you have always insisted had to be part of your marriage?"

"I'm not sure. I think perhaps love is involved, but there

is one big obstacle standing in my way."

Margaret tilted her head in question. "And that would be?"

Sybil wrinkled her nose. "Lady MacBride."

"Oh." Margaret sat back and shook her head. "Not a very pleasant woman, I'm afraid."

"Yes. Quite true. She has been most unpleasant to me ever since I arrived." Lady MacBride had also extended her poor manners to Margaret. Sybil had been embarrassed several times at the curt responses she'd given both to her and Margaret. Most times it was when Liam was not around to hear her.

"Well, you wouldn't be marrying the woman."

"Come now, Margaret, you must know when women are to live in the same house, no matter how large, if there is animosity between them, it can make for a very troublesome life."

Margaret gave her a slow nod. "I am afraid you have the right of it in that regard. What does Liam say about her?"

"He has indicated that she has a deep-seated dislike of all things English. He's even said he would speak to her, but I really don't want to cause problems between mother and son."

"Nonsense. Liam does not strike me as the type of man who is led about by his mother. I think you are giving this situation too much importance."

"Perhaps." Sybil twisted her fingers. "There is something else."

Margaret regarded her with raised eyebrows.

"You seem happy, Margaret, truly you do. But I must say I don't know for certain if I could be content away from my family, my country. Things are different here. If I marry Liam my children will be raised in the Scottish way."

She clasped Margaret's hands. "I'm sorry. I shouldn't have said that. You must think me horrid, since your children will be raised Scottish."

"I know. And I have thought about it. But if you truly love someone, nothing else really matters."

"So your marriage has become a love match?"

Margaret giggled, her face a bright red.

Sybil smiled. Well, that would certainly make a difference. However, while she cared a great deal for Liam, her heart was still a few steps away from the word *love*.

They both sat in silence for a few moments as Margaret composed herself. "What of his sisters? They seem to be sweet girls."

"Oh, they are wonderful. I miss my own sisters so much, and they have definitely filled a bit of that hole in my heart." After her initial reticence, Alanna had become as open and likeable as Catriona. The girl had even come to her for advice on how to have their maid dress her hair for her very first ball. Both girls had looked exquisite. Liam would have his hands full keeping the men away from them once they reached their come-out.

"See. There you have it. Three out of four people love you. You'll just have to learn to ignore the woman." She paused. "And I can almost guarantee that once a babe is on the way, she will change her attitude."

Sybil's face heated again, concerned that a babe might already be on the way. If that were to happen, the choice would be taken away from her. She really must rein in her lust for the man and not allow him anymore privileges until they got this marriage thing settled. Hoping Margaret hadn't noticed her blush, she said, "I hope you're right. But I'm not as certain as you are. Don't forget the babe would have English blood."

Yes, a child with both English and Scottish blood. Shouldn't she prefer to raise him in the English way? She sighed. All of this had her going around in circles.

A scratch at Sybil's bedchamber door drew their attention.

Bessie entered at their summons. "I'm sorry to interrupt, my lady. But The McKinnon asked me to remind Lady McKinnon that her bedchamber is down the corridor."

"Oh, heavens." Margaret jumped up, covering her reddened cheeks with her hands.

"It seems your husband is feeling a bit lonely, Margaret." Sybil laughed at her friend's distress. It appeared Margaret had made an excellent adjustment to the marriage bed.

"Yes. I believe you are right." Margaret bent and gave Sybil a hug. "I will see you at breakfast."

"Yes. If your husband allows you out of bed."

"Sybil!" Margaret turned and fled from the room to the sound of Sybil's laughter.

Chapter Sixteen

Three days after the ball Lady MacBride entered the library, her lips tightened. "Ye wish to speak with me?"

Liam put down the pen he was writing with and stood. "Good morning to ye, Mum." He waved at the chair in front of his massive wooden desk. "Yes. Please have a seat."

She fiddled with her skirts, avoiding his eyes. "Ye need to make it quick, I have many things to attend to."

Duncan and Margaret had left after dinner the prior evening. Once again, his mum had excused herself right from the dinner table, leaving Margaret and Sybil staring at each other at the woman's lack of manners to her guests, and Liam fuming at her behavior.

The ball had been a success, everyone wishing The McKinnon and his wife happiness and a long, fruitful marriage. Everyone except Mum. Luckily, it appeared no one in his clan had noticed her lack of enthusiasm.

Liam smiled, remembering the broad winks and nudges

he'd received from clansmen hinting that it was near time for him to join his friend in matrimony. Not too subtle glances and nods were tossed in Sybil's direction, whom he'd made sure spent most of the evening beside him.

But now the time had come to speak to Mum about her refusal to accept the way things were.

He remembered his da having problems with Mum, also. As much as they loved the woman, and thanked the good Lord for her love and devotion to her family, she could be a trial with her stubbornness.

He agreed with his clan. It was time to marry and begin producing bairns. And he would have no other than Lady Sybil Lacey. He steeled himself to face the biggest challenge to his happiness. The conversation he was about to have was not one he'd been looking forward to.

His heart told him that Sybil was ready to accept his proposal. Besides which, they were moving into dangerous waters with their inability to keep their hands off each other. The matter had to be settled.

Liam rested his elbow on the arm of his chair, his fingers cupping his chin. "Ye ken I hold Lady Sybil in great regard."

His mum brushed invisible lint from her apron. "Foolishness."

"Nay, Mum. Not foolishness. I've asked the lass to marry me, and I believe she is ready to accept."

Her face flushed, Mum pushed back her chair and stood, her hands fisted at her sides. "Nay! I've said it before, and I say it now. I will never accept a Sassenach daughter-in-law. Ye need to look for a Scottish lass to wed."

As much as he wanted to shake the stubborn woman, he managed to remain calm. He would prefer not turning this into a battle. However, he'd given his mum enough time to adjust to the inevitable. He loved Sybil, intended to marry her, and get her with child as often as he could. And nothing was going to stop him. Not even the woman who had given him life.

"Ye need to put aside yer prejudices. Lady Sybil is a wonderful woman. She is smart, kind and from what I have seen since she arrived here, very patient with yer rudeness."

"She's fooled ye. Once ye make her yer wife she'll turn on ye. Just like the English have always done. She'll make ye miserable yer whole life, always looking for more and more, wantin' everyone to wait on her, lookin' night and day fer ways to spend yer coin."

Liam dragged his palm down his face. This was not going to be easy. He'd been fooled, all right. Fooled into believing his mum would have seen the goodness in the lass by now. She'd been here for weeks and had remained ever pleasant to Mum, even though the woman had treated her shamefully. The time had come to take a stand and let her ken how things were going to be.

"Ye mistake my intentions in speaking with ye. I am not seeking permission. I dinna need it, nor want it. Lady Sybil is my choice for a bride, and I have every reason to believe she will have me. I am giving ye the courtesy of kenning ahead of time, and asking ye to be helpful to the lass in planning the wedding."

Her face grew red to the point where he feared she would suffer apoplexy. "I won't be planning a wedding for a Sassenach. If ye want to make a fool of yerself with the Englishwoman, ye won't be seeing my hand in it."

He stood, towering over her, both their bodies shaking with rage. "Woman, 'tis the end of the discussion. I am yer laird, and I order ye to cease your blathering and prepare to make peace with the lass. I won't have ye causing unhappiness." He stopped to catch his breath, trying very hard to rein in his anger. "If ye insist on making things miserable for everyone, ye will find yerself living beyond these walls."

His mum reared back as if slapped. "Ye would put yer own mother aside for a Sassenach?"

"Nay. I would put my own mother aside for my *wife*." He softened his expression and reached out to her, but she turned away from him. "I just ask ye to give the lass a chance."

She stubbornly shook her head and then waved her finger at him, much like she had done when he had been a lad and in trouble. "Ye will regret the day ye turned yer back on your Scottish ancestors who are surely today spinning in their graves. Mayhap ye can forget Culloden, but I cannot. Nor how they took our land and tossed us off our farms to starve. We suffered at the hands of the woman ye would make the mum of yer bairns. 'Tis a sad day."

"By the saints, woman! Ye are speaking history. None of us were even born then. 'Tis time to put yer hatred aside and begin to see what yer future daughter-in-law is like."

She waved her finger at him. "Ye had yer own dislike of the English all yer life. What has this lass done that changed ye? Or should I take a guess at what she did *for* ye that has ye so bewitched?"

If he'd ever come close to actually striking a woman it was at this very moment. Helping to rein in his anger at his mum's wicked accusation was the fact that he and Sybil had indeed engaged in improper behavior. But 'twas more than lust that drove him.

"Ye shall not speak of the lass that way ever again!"

He took a calming breath. "She is different from the English. And if ye can't see it, then yer blind."

For a minute he thought she intended to continue the argument. Then with a tilt of her chin and a smug look she said, "Ye might still have another chance to wed the right woman."

He narrowed his eyes. "What are ye blathering about now?"

"Ye were betrothed to the McLaughlin lass when ye were a bairn."

He hadn't thought of The McLaughlin, nor his daughter for years. He'd still been a lad when the two lairds had stood before a magistrate over a dispute that broke the friendship the men had shared for years. "Aye, And da canceled that betrothal when he and The McLaughlin had a falling out. That was years ago, woman."

"Aye years ago. Since the matter at the heart of the problem has since been resolved, the bad feelings between our clans is naught."

He didn't like where this conversation was headed. "What is yer point?"

"Before ye went to the McKinnon's wedding, I sent a letter to The McLaughlin, telling him ye were searching for a wife, and he should re-consider his daughter, Anise."

"Ye did what? Ye had no right!" Blood pounded in his head so fiercely he thought it would spew out his ears.

She drew herself up. "I am yer mother. I had every right to see that you upheld your responsibility to the clan."

"My responsibility to the clan is mine. And yer attempt to manage my life is for naught since the McLaughlin lass has probably married and has bairns tugging at her skirts."

"Nay. She was indeed wed, several years ago, but her

husband died and her da is anxious to see her wed once again."

"I wish the man luck, but he will not be wedding the lass to me."

"Ye can at least take a look at her."

"Nay. Ye will send a note to the man and tell him I am about to be married to someone else and wish him well with Anise."

When she crossed her arms over her chest and glared at him, he said, "Ye Laird is speaking to ye, woman."

"As you wish, *my laird*." She turned on her heel and left the room.

Feeling as if all the air had been let out of his lungs, he collapsed into his chair and leaning his head back closed his eyes. But 'twas done. He'd told her what she needed to do.

• • •

"Why won't you tell me where we are going?" Sybil tugged on her gloves as Liam hurried her out the door.

"'Tis a surprise. I've been busy all morning with correspondence, now I wish to have some time with my lady."

The afternoon air was warm, making her quite comfortable in just her gown and a light pelisse. She tied the wide ribbons of her bonnet and breathed deeply of the clean, fresh air. The hills were covered in deep and light green shades, reminiscent of a counterpane she'd had on her bed as a young girl. The Highlands was truly a beautiful place.

They wandered along, Liam pointing out various places he'd played as a child, obviously very fond of his country and home.

He gestured toward a gnarled oak tree that seemed to end in the clouds. "'Twas there Duncan and I climbed to the top and were too afraid to come down. The lad and I spent the entire night up there."

"All night?"

He nodded. "The next morning my da and Laird McKinnon had clansmen from both castles scouring the countryside looking for us. And when they found us, well, 'twas a long punishment, that time."

"How old were you?"

"About six summers."

She shivered. "I would be so frightened if a child of mine were missing all night." Just the thought of sweet little Robert, Drake and Penelope's boy, being away all night was enough to make her heart beat double time. In England such a thing would not happen. Children were not given such freedom at tender ages.

Liam took her hand in his, and they strolled a bit more until they reached a pond. The water was clear and crisp, with sunlight casting diamond-like sparkles on the water. Another enormous tree, with a rope dangling from one of the branches, hung over the water.

"Let me guess," Sybil said. "You and Duncan would swing from that rope and land in the pond?"

"Aye. It sounds as though ye may have done the same thing as a lass."

"We did. Drake snuck a rope from papa's garden shed and hung the line. He and Joseph, his best friend, tried to keep it a secret from the rest of us, but my sister, Abigail, ferreted out the information. They never had a moment's peace after that.

"You know, sometimes I find it hard to believe we are all grown up. Joseph is now married to Abigail, Drake is married to his beloved botanist, and Marion's husband is back home. It doesn't seem all that long ago that we were all children, running around our estate grounds, getting into trouble."

"And one day I hope to have our bairns running around here." He kissed the back of her hand. "Just say the word, lass."

Deciding silence was the best answer, she continued on. Soon they arrived at the top of a hill, and Sybil gasped as they crested the peak. Before them was the sea, an angry expanse of blue-black water that pounded on the huge rocks, spewing foam high into the air. The salt air blew into their faces, whipping Liam's hair into his face.

As he stood there surveying the area, his bright green eyes taking in the sight, his massive shoulders an outline against the deep blue sky, he looked much like how she imagined a Scottish warrior from the medieval ages looked. All he was missing was a sporran, broadsword, and his kilt.

The fluttering began in her lower parts as she studied him. Strong chin, high cheekbones, straight nose. With his feet planted apart, his hands fisted on his hips, he was every Scottish combatant from the beginning of time. He turned to her and flashed the grin that never failed to melt her insides.

"Aye, one of my favorite spots." He took a step down a rocky path toward the sea, then turned and extended his hand. "Come with me, darlin'. Ye need to get closer to the water."

"Is it safe?"

"I would never let anything happen to ye, lass." Her

heart skipped a beat as he towered over her, watching her with those deep green eyes that had the power to take her breath away. There was so much in his expression that convinced her that this was the right man, at the right time, in the right place. The man she'd waited for. She loved The MacBride, and whatever problems they might face in the future, hopefully they would do it together.

Then like a cloud passing over the sun, she realized no matter how optimistic her thoughts, a niggling of doubt always arose. She was English, Liam was Scottish, and his mother heartily disapproved of any match between them. Could she put aside her own prejudices and raise a child in the Scottish ways? Would they fight the war between England and Scotland in their own bedchamber?

Gripping her hand tightly, he led her down the path to a small beach a short distance from the rugged rocks. Her shoes sank into the wet sand, making a sucking sound when she walked. But it was worth the discomfort to feel the spray of water on her face and inhale the salt and brine.

She gripped the ribbons of her bonnet as she fought the wind to keep it on her head, and her pelisse around her body. The harshness of the ocean as the waves pounded the rocks heightened her senses, bringing with it an excitement she'd never felt before. She stopped for a moment to watch nature's breathtaking show. Without a word, Liam bent and scooped her into his arms.

"What are you doing?" She laughed at the combination of salt, sand, and sunshine. And the man who held her in his powerful arms. No, nothing could go wrong with Liam by her side.

"Yer such a wee little thing, I'm afraid the wind will

carry ye away from me. I'm going to deliver ye to that rock yonder." He gestured with his chin to a large boulder that looked like a seat had been carved out in the middle of it. She wrapped her arms around his neck and laid her head on his shoulder. Peace settled over her. This was right.

Once he had her firmly on the rock, he grinned and pulled something from his pocket. What was this man up to now? Liam cleared his throat, and all of a sudden his expression grew thoughtful and—scared? Her heart filled at the vulnerable look on his face.

Staring directly at her, he took her hand in his and went down on one knee. He kissed her fingertips and said, "Lass, I've asked ye this a few times before, but now I'm wanting an answer. I love ye, Lady Sybil, and wish more than anything in the world to have ye for my wife. Unless I've lost all my ability to judge people, I think ye care for me, too. So, one more time. Will ye marry me?"

Her throat thickened, and her eyes filled with tears. How could she have ever thought this man was a barbarian? The love and hope on his face filled her with such love for him in return that she couldn't even form the word he so wanted to hear. Instead, she merely nodded her acceptance, two tears tracking down her cheeks.

Liam carefully slid a ruby and diamond ring onto her finger. "'Twas my grandmother's. It came to me after she died."

Sybil studied the beautiful ring through watery eyes. "It is exquisite."

Standing, he pulled her to her feet and cupped her cheeks. *Tha gaol agam ort,"* he whispered before he slowly bent his head and took her lips in a soft, gentle kiss.

The wind buffeted them as they stood on the rock, the beauty of the Highlands on one side, the rough angry sea on the other. A fine mist of cold salt water sprayed them, but Sybil was warmed from her toes to her head by her betrothed's kiss. "What did you say? Was that Gaelic?"

He ran his finger down her cheek. "Yes. I said 'I love you.'"

"I love you, too."

"*Tha gaol agam ort-fhèin*."

She gave him a questioning glance.

"That means I love you, too, in Gaelic."

"Oh. *Tha gaol agam ort-fhèin*" She stumbled slightly, but it came out at least similar to what he'd said.

"Verra good, my lady. I'll make a Scottish lass out of ye yet."

"And is that so important?"

"'Twould help." He grinned and winked at her.

She raised her chin. "Indeed?"

"Ach, I'm teasing ye."

He wrapped his arms around her and held her close. "I think we should get married tomorrow."

"What?" She leaned back so she could look into his eyes. "Tomorrow?"

"Aye. Now that I have yer consent, I don't want to give ye time to change yer mind."

"I won't change my mind." She shook her head. "But I want a proper wedding. I need my family to be here."

He sighed and tucked a loose curl back into her bonnet. "Aye. I ken you would."

The wind had picked up, chilling them both. Sybil shivered and burrowed into Liam's warmth. She inhaled the familiar and comforting scents of Liam. Her man. She smiled into the wool of his jacket.

"Come, lass. Yer getting chilled." He hopped down from the rock and reached up for her. Wrapping his hands around her waist, he swung her down, kissing her as she slid down his body. "Ach, lass. We need to find a fast way for yer family to travel here. I want ye in my bed, where I can keep ye verra warm."

Sybil flushed at the fond memories of how Liam kept her warm. It would be interesting to make love in a bed, since both times had been on the library floor.

Holding hands, they climbed up the slight incline until they were blocked from the sea by the hill they'd crested on their way to the water. Away from the ocean the wind subsided, making the walk back warmer and quite pleasant.

"I will tell my mum and sisters at dinner that ye accepted my proposal."

One final hurdle to climb, it seemed. How would her future mother-in-law take this news? Until now it seemed she'd had no use for her, and all of Sybil's attempts to make the woman warm toward her had failed. But she would not allow Lady MacBride to ruin her happiness.

She glanced up at Liam to find him staring at her. "What?"

"I'm thinking of how I can sneak into yer bedchamber tonight."

"Liam, no! That's improper."

His eyebrows rose. "The library floor is more proper?"

"No. We cannot continue that until we're married."

"Ach, lass. If ye think I can stay away from ye now that I ken ye are mine, yer sadly mistaken."

• • •

Dinner was a quiet affair. Once Liam made his announcement, both of his sisters squealed with delight, jumping up in a most unladylike manner, each giving Sybil a sisterly hug. His mum remained silent, not making any comments.

"When is the wedding?" Catriona bounced up and down on her seat, her bright eyes full of excitement.

"Lady Sybil must write to her family first, and we need to give them time to travel here."

"Actually, Liam," Sybil said, "Now that I've thought about this, my sister Abigail just had twins in February." She began counting on her fingers. "My brother and his wife also had a baby girl in February, and my sister Marion was expecting her baby around now. She most likely has a newborn child herself."

"Ach, lass. Yer family is exploding."

"Indeed. But only my sister, Sarah will be able to travel any distance. I would never want my wedding to not include her."

"We can travel to England and marry there."

"No, Liam," Alanna said. "You must marry here so our clan can witness their laird's marriage. 'Tis tradition, right, Mum?"

All eyes swung to the one person who had left herself out of the conversation. "It matters naught. 'Tis the laird's choice. Let *my laird* decide what he wants to do. 'Tis his decision." Feigning indifference, she returned to her meal.

"I have a suggestion. Why don't we marry here and then travel to England to visit with yer family?" Anything to get Sybil right where he wanted her as soon as possible. In his bed and in his arms.

Sybil seemed to consider the idea. “That might be the best solution.”

“Aye. Then ’tis settled. We will have the wedding in three weeks.” He peered at mum who continued to pretend the conversation was not taking place. “Can I ask ye to help with the wedding?”

She placed her fork neatly at the side of her plate. “Of course, *my laird*.” She pushed back her chair and stood. “I will go immediately to the kitchen and work out the menu with Mrs. MacDougal, *my laird*.” With a slight nod she turned and left the room.

Liam dropped his head into his hands and groaned.

Chapter Seventeen

Two weeks passed in a flurry of wedding preparations. To Liam's amazement his mum actually did help quite a bit with the arrangements. While not actually being pleasant, nevertheless, she did what needed to be done to make sure all would run smoothly on his wedding day.

His wedding day. It couldn't come soon enough. True to her word, Sybil had barred him from her bedchamber and refused to remain in the library after his sisters had retired for the evening. His frustration grew each day. This time next week he would be a married man and more than happy to retire to their bedchamber each night right from the dinner table as his mum continued to do.

While the women fussed about the wedding, he'd spent his time getting estate matters in order so he and Sybil could take sufficient time to travel to England and spend time with her kin. He hoped her family didn't hold the same disdain for the Scots as his mum did for the English. However, based on what she'd told him of them, he doubted he would be met with anything but acceptance.

A scratch at his office door drew his attention from his musings about the very wicked things he intended to do with his bride very soon. "Yes. Come."

His mum stood at the doorway, a look of pleasure on her face such as he hadn't seen in a while. In fact, not since Sybil had arrived. She moved forward, her hands behind her back. An unexplained nugget of fear settled in his stomach. *What was the woman up to now?*

"I wanted to speak with ye about yer wedding plans."

Liam nodded to the chair in front of his desk.

His mum settled herself, drawing out a piece of foolscap from behind her back and rested it in her lap. "Everything is ready."

"I am glad to hear it." He tensed further. Something was wrong. Verra wrong. He knew his mum well. If she was this happy, it didn't bode well for him.

She smiled brightly. "There will need to be one change, however."

Liam shifted in his seat, trying to relax his muscles. "What are ye up to woman? I don't like the look on yer face, and you obviously have something yer dying to tell me. So stop playing games and speak."

"It seems the change will be yer bride." The joy on her face as she took the foolscap from her lap and placed it onto his desk knotted his stomach. She was entirely too happy.

With shaky hands he picked up the paper and skimmed the words. 'Twas a letter from The McLaughlin assuring Lady MacBride that he was thrilled to once again join his daughter, Anise, and Laird MacBride. He and the lass were on their way to Bedlay Castle.

He tossed the paper aside with a sense of relief. They'd already gone over this. "Nay. I instructed you to write to the man and tell him I would not renew the betrothal agreement."

She sat forward. "What do ye mean, nay? The honor of our entire clan rests with you fulfilling the betrothal agreement." She gestured with her chin toward the letter.

Liam ran his fingers through his hair. "There is no agreement, and I will not abide ye taking these matters into yer own hands and refusing to honor what yer laird ordered. I have made my choice, and 'tis not Anise McLaughlin. I will write to him and explain I am already betrothed and will marry within a week's time."

"And make a liar out of yer mum? I told him ye were in the market for a bride."

"How many times do ye need to hear me say ye have no right to interfere with my life?"

Lady MacBride stabbed the paper on his desk with her finger. "Ye canna stop him from coming. Laird McLaughlin and yer bride are on their way here."

Jumping up from his chair, Liam shouted, "My bride is right here at Bedlay. If ye refuse to send a messenger to intercept them, then I shall move up my wedding to the morn, and ye can greet the man by yerself with the news that me and my bride are on our honeymoon."

His mum sneered. "'Twas bad enough when ye decided to betrothe yerself to a Sassenach, but I will not sit by and watch ye dishonor yer clan by embarrassing me and then tossing everything Scottish in ye to the wind. 'Tis an awkward spot ye put me in with The McLaughlin."

He waved his hand in dismissal. "Ye got yerself into this mess. Ye can get yerself out of it."

His mother's shoulders slumped. "Ach lad. Yer not giving this enough thought. If ye have yer way, ye'll be raising a passel of English brats. Anise McLaughlin is a good, Scottish lass. She will give ye strong lads."

He hit his chest with his thumb. "Nay. My bairns will be Scottish, naught English." Any lads and lasses of his would be Scottish in name and heritage. He'd make certain they understood that their sweet mother notwithstanding, the English were a nasty lot who had persecuted the Scots for decades.

"Half English!" she shouted.

"Nay! Scottish." He leaned forward. "My love for the English is no more than yers." He pounded his fist on the desk. "My bairns will be Scottish. Do ye hear me woman? Naught English. They will be raised in the Scottish tradition and never be called Sassenach!"

• • •

Sybil stopped abruptly at the door to the library. Recently returning from her walk in the garden with Catriona and Alanna, she'd been drawn to the library door by the sound of Lady MacBride's voice raised in anger. Hating that she was eavesdropping, nevertheless she didn't make her presence known.

Anise McLaughlin?

All the blood drained from Sybil's face as she heard Liam's declaration. She pushed open the door with her fingertips. Liam and his mother glared at each other, both in a combative stance.

"Liam?" Her voice rasped.

Flushed-face, his head jerked toward the door as he regarded her. His eyes grew wide. "Ach lass. I dinna ken you were there."

She raised her chin. "Apparently not. However, it would have been hard not to hear you, anyway. I am sure my brother, the very *English* Duke of Manchester heard you all the way in London."

Lady MacBride's lip curled as she strolled toward Sybil. "Now ye know what yer betrothed thinks of yer English, *Lady Sybil.*" She swept from the room, holding her skirts close as if to avoid touching her.

Liam held out his hand. "Lass, I was angry. The woman does that to me. I dinna mean it."

"Yes, you did." She moved farther into the room, her fists at her side, her chin quivering with emotion. "And, *my laird*, do you think I would be happy to raise my *English* children as Scottish? Do you think you are the only one with pride?"

How dare he impugn the English? Here he was professing love for her when all the time he hated everything that represented what she was. Her heritage was as important to her as his was to him. She should have known that his heart was so full of his clan, his mother, and his way of life, that there was no room for her. Or for any children they might have had who would be half English.

He moved around the desk and stood in front of her. "I think we both need to calm down."

Her eyes filled with tears, but she refused to let them fall. "No. It appears your mum has already selected a woman for you who will *give ye strong lads*. We have made a grave mistake." As if seeing clearly for the first time in weeks, she realized his disdain for her when they'd first met made his profession of love all lies. How could she have believed he had actually put aside his dislike and distrust of an entire nation of people? For her?

She'd been a fool. Closing her eyes briefly at the pain of her dreams shattering, she turned and headed for the door.

"Sybil."

She shook her head, and held up her hand when he started toward her. "I will have Bessie pack my belongings. If you will notify your driver to prepare your carriage, I should like to leave as soon as I am ready. Then you can prepare for your wedding to the Scottish woman." She raised her chin. "You do remember you promised my brother you would provide transportation home when I was ready to leave?"

He rested his hands on his hips and peered at her through shuttered eyes. "Aye. I remember. But I think ye should give yerself time to calm down so we can discuss this."

She smiled sadly, her eyes burning from where the tears had gathered. "There is nothing to discuss. I believe everything worth saying has been stated. Quite clearly and at the top of your lungs." She hurried from the room, the knot in her throat choking her.

Once she entered her bedchamber, she walked to the window, looking out at the beautiful Scottish Highlands. Finally the tears spilled from her eyes and dripped from her chin to land on the window sill. It had all been a dream. She didn't belong here, and Liam had just confirmed it. Apparently Lady MacBride had done an excellent job of tainting Liam's view of everything and everyone English.

She rubbed her hands up and down her arms, trying to erase the chill that had settled on her. Never in her life had she been so miserable. She'd finally found the man she'd been holding out for; someone to love, who loved her in return. Unfortunately, there was the little matter of a deep seated prejudice against her and her people.

"That's what I get for trusting a *Scottish barbarian* with my heart," she murmured.

She slipped the ring off her finger and placed it on the pillow on her bed, then went in search of Bessie.

• • •

"Has she said anything yet?" Mary asked.

"Nothing." Sarah sighed.

Sybil listened against the closed breakfast room door, trying to garner the strength to walk into the room and face her family once again. Since she'd returned from Scotland they'd all tip-toed around her.

Two long weeks had passed, and she'd smiled when she was heartbroken, laughed when she wanted to cry. But she had fooled no one. Her surprised and unannounced return to her country home had been met with joy. At first. Then her family began their solicitous attentions. Sybil found it impossible to talk about Liam, even to her beloved twin. Her pain was too raw, too new.

Her anger had slowly faded over time, replaced with a longing that hurt. She still hadn't reached the point where she could get past even ten minutes without thinking about him. About the fact that he was most likely married to the woman his mum was so determined to have him wed. A woman much more suited to Bedlay and the MacBride clan.

She tried shopping, visiting friends, afternoon teas, but

nothing worked. No matter where she was or what she was doing, a scene would flash through her mind of them together. Then her heart would ache so much it would double her over.

Forcing cheerfulness, she opened the door and entered the room. "Good morning."

"Good morning," they all chorused.

Her brother, Drake, his wife, Penelope, her sisters Sarah and Mary, along with her mother, the Dowager Duchess of Manchester, all returned bright smiles. She moved to her chair as though she was the pathetic heroine in a bad play. The difference was, an actress playing her part would leave the stage and resume her normal life. Sybil's life would never be normal again.

Damn the Scot.

She almost giggled at the idea of asking her family, *How does one recover from a heart so broken that the pieces have scattered like dust in the wind?* That would surely make for interesting breakfast conversation.

Drake had tried several times to talk to her about her trip, but she had brushed him off. She'd been holding herself together for so long she feared if she uttered one word about Liam or their time together out loud, the floodgates would open and she would never stop crying.

"Mary and I are going to the village, would you like to come?" Sarah placed her hand on Sybil's. "We thought we'd go to the bookstore and see what new books have come in."

Nay, lass. I ken which one the bookstore is. 'Tis the one with the books in the window.

Unbidden, the tears came. Without a sound she sat very still as thick drops seeped from her eyes, dripping from her chin onto her lap. She closed her eyes, trying to stem the tide, but it didn't work. "Excuse me," she mumbled. Pushing her chair back, she quickly moved to the door and raced up to her bedchamber.

It would be another long day.

• • •

Liam awoke with a throbbing headache, ready to face another day full of misery. He'd been gone from Bedlay for three weeks. Three weeks of seeking the bottom of the next bottle of whiskey and trying his best not to beat someone senseless.

He rolled over and stared at the ceiling. All he saw was Sybil's face. The small room he'd been in for three weeks now closed in on him. It was time to return home and face The McLaughlin and Anise. Do his duty. Uphold the honor of his clan.

Once Sybil had climbed into his carriage to journey home, still stiff with anger, he'd vaulted onto Cadeym and ridden for hours with no particular destination in mind. Just as the sun had begun its descent he had found himself at an inn, miles from Bedlay Castle. Not interested in where he was, he ordered a bottle of whiskey sent up to his room. Aside from the occasional meal tray, over the past three weeks he'd merely indulged himself in pity.

Sybil had thought all Scots were whiskey swizzlers and bar brawlers. He gently touched the bruise under his eye from the fight he'd had last night when he'd finally ventured from his room and had taken insult on something an Englishman had said about the Scots. Well, a swizzler and brawler is what he had apparently turned into.

Why he'd blurted out that stupid comment about the *Sassenach* while in the middle of his argument with mum angered him still.

He'd lived with his mum's hatred of the English, but he genuinely thought the hatred had not seeped into his bones. Were he to be honest with himself, he did not feel the dislike his mum felt for the Sassenach. He loved Sybil. It was that simple. He didn't care if she was a dairy maid, or an American, even.

He would have been happy to teach his bairns about their English family, just as he would have liked to tell them about their Scottish ancestry. But he'd lost his chance when he'd let his temper get the better of his common sense.

He swung his legs over the edge of the bed and held his aching head in his hands. A bath, breakfast, and a slow ride home was the order for the day. Best to get it over with.

The sight that greeted him as he crested the hill leading to Bedlay didn't inspire the pride and joy it normally did. All he saw was an old castle that would never be filled with the sound of Sybil's laughter, or the bairns he'd planned to have with her. Little lasses with long brown curls and sparkling whiskey-colored eyes. Half-English and half-Scottish.

Taking a deep breath, he rode the rest of the way, stopping at the stable to leave Cadeym.

"Good morning, my laird. 'Twas a long trip ye took this time."

"Aye." He handed the reins over to Angus, the old man who'd been stable master since he'd been a lad. "Have our guests arrived?"

"Aye, Laird. About a week ago."

Liam nodded and headed to the castle. The enticing aroma of fresh baked bread greeted him as he entered, restoring his appetite for the first time in weeks. He passed empty rooms as he wandered through the lower floor and then entered the kitchen.

"Praise the Lord, the laird has returned!" Mrs. MacDougal turned from the pot over the fireplace she'd been tending to, a huge smile on her rounded face.

"Aye. And 'tis starving I am."

"Well, sit yerself right down, and I'll fix ye a fine plate of stew."

"And some of that wonderful bread I smell."

She bustled around the room, scooping stew into a bowl, then placing it in front of him, along with several thick slices of bread and butter.

After he'd had his fill, he pushed his empty bowl away and asked, "Where is my mum?"

The cheerful woman carried a cup of tea to the table where he sat and settled in across from him. "She's been busy entertaining her guests. A sweet lass, that Anise McLaughlin. Verra quiet, fearful, sort of. Not like Lady Sybil, that one. Your mum brought her to the kitchen to see how it all works but she dinna seem too interested. Spent most of her time twisting her fingers and staring at the ground."

Liam sat back and crossed his arms over his chest. He thought of the lass his mum had sent for, and then his mind wandered toward Sybil. Her face, her spirit, her love of life. The way she smiled at him, how she made him feel when he held her close. Her kisses and laughter.

A fire started low in his belly and tightened his muscles. His heart pounded, and a burst of energy like he'd never felt before raced through him, jolting him from his chair as if booted from behind. The shroud of despair that had kept him company for weeks fell like broken glass at his feet. He was not a quitter. By the saints! What the hell had he done?

Mrs. MacDougal jumped as he banged his fist into a wall and let out with a fine string of curses. She studied him for a minute. "Laird, it sounds as if ye have finally come to yer senses."

He rubbed his sore knuckles. "Aye, Mrs. MacDougal. I have indeed come to my senses. Now 'tis the time to set things to rights."

She gave him a wide grin, revealing a missing front tooth. "I like the look in yer eyes, Laird."

He kissed the woman on the top of her head and strode from the kitchen in search of mum. Why the devil had he let Sybil leave? He should have physically thrown her over his shoulder and hauled her upstairs to lock her in his bedchamber until he'd convinced her he'd made a huge mistake. He should have not let her out of his bed until she understood that what he'd yelled in a moment of anger was not how he truly felt.

Sounds of conversation drifted from the parlor, and he followed the path to the voices. His mum sat, embroidery in her hand, instructing Anise, as The McLaughlin looked on.

"There he is now, Laird." His mum stood and greeted him with a bright smile as if she hadn't torn his life apart only a few weeks ago. "'Tis so glad I am yer home, lad. I told The McLaughlin how yer were called away to deal with a problem with the clan."

He swallowed his anger and turned to The McLaughlin. "My Laird." Then he walked to Anise and greeted her, never having laid eyes on the lass before. She was slight, with golden hair fashioned in braids wrapped demurely around her head. She glanced up at him briefly, her sky blue eyes casting back down toward her lap as she fidgeted with her fingers.

Although of a pleasant countenance, she was not his Sybil. This was a lass who could disappear in a room full of people. Sybil would be at the center, laughing, joking, and trying hard not to notice his heated looks. Anise McLaughlin looked as if she were terrified of him.

Taking a deep breath, he turned to her father. "I request that ye grant us privacy so I may speak with yer daughter."

"Aye. Yes, yes," his mum said grinning. She picked up her embroidery and hustled The McLaughlin out of the room.

If he hadn't been so angry with her, he would have laughed at what she must have thought was his imminent proposal to the lass.

Once the door closed, he turned to Anise. "Have ye had a pleasant visit while I've been gone?"

She nodded her head, keeping her focus on her lap. He clasped his hands behind his back and paced. "Lass. Ye are a sweet, bonnie girl and would make any man proud to call ye wife."

The distinct sound of a whimper came from her direction. This would indeed go much better if she at least looked at him. He moved toward her, thinking to go down on his knee so he could see her face, but decided since the lass was expecting a proposal, that was not the best position to put himself into.

"Anise. Can ye at least look at me, please?"

Slowly she raised her head, chewing her lip, her eyes as

wide as Mrs. MacDougal's oat cakes.

"Are ye all right, lass?"

She shrugged.

Time was wasting that he could be on his way to England. Best to get this over with and depart. "I hate to disappoint ye, and I hope not to hurt yer feelings, but the fact of the matter is, my mum overstepped herself. I am not prepared to make ye an offer of marriage."

For the first time since he'd entered the room, she looked at him, a smile spreading across her face. "Yer not?"

"Nay. I am betrothed to another, and my mum had no right to ask yer father to bring ye here."

She hopped up and grabbed his hand. "Oh, thank you, my laird. Thank you so much." The wee lass threw her arms around his neck and gave him a large, rather sloppy kiss on his cheek.

He drew back, grinning at her unexpected response "Well, 'tis happy I am that yer so relieved."

"I am. Truly, I am. My da wouldna listen to me. He was so anxious to join our clans, he refused Alfred's request for my hand."

"Alfred?"

"Yes. He is a wonderful man. He loves me, and I love him. He has his own land and raises sheep." Her words fought with her lungs for breath.

A slight scratch at the door drew their attention. The McLaughlin and his mum entered, both grinning from ear to ear. "So, lad have ye set a date?" his mum said.

Liam looked at Anise and they both burst into laughter.

The McLaughlin and his mum threw them curious glances. "And what is so funny?"

"Sit down, the both of ye." Liam motioned to Anise to take a seat as well, but he remained standing, his hands clasped behind his back. "There will be no wedding between me and Anise." He raised his hand when his mum opened her mouth to speak. "Dinna interrupt."

Liam turned to The McLaughlin. "I apologize to ye, Laird. My mum overstepped herself. I am betrothed to another woman."

"What is this?" The man glared at his mum. "Ye told me the lad wanted a wife. Ye invited us here to make the final arrangements and have a wedding. My daughter is verra upset at this turn of events."

"Nay, da." Her face pale, Anise jumped in. "I am not upset. I told ye many times Alfred has asked for my hand, and it is he who I wish to wed."

"Why do ye think ye can just fancy someone and marry them?" Lady MacBride scowled at the two of them. "Ye neither one have loyalty to yer clans."

Liam ignored his mum and addressed The McLaughlin. "'Tis sorry I am for all the trouble my mum put you through. But I will not be marrying yer daughter, and I sincerely hope ye will grant yer permission and blessing to Anise and her Alfred to marry."

The McLaughlin looked at his daughter and his expression softened. "Aye, lass. If it's Alfred yer wanting, then let's be on our way." He stood and addressed Lady MacBride. "'Tis time for us to acknowledge what we think is best for our children is not always what they want."

His mum huffed and crossed her arms over her chest.

Liam motioned to his mum. There was still one more thing he had to do before he left for England. "Mum, I will see ye in the library, please."

Her brows drawn together, she followed him. He motioned for her to take a seat and he settled in the chair across from her.

She went on the attack immediately. "I canna believe ye would embarrass me so in front of The McLaughlin. Yer making a grave mistake. Why are ye thinking with yer man parts instead of yer brain?"

Despite the anger that rose in him, he waved her question away. He would not allow her to drag him into an argument when he was anxious to leave. "'Tis a mean thing ye did, mum. When we are finished with this conversation, I am headed to England to bring Sybil back here if she will have me."

"Nay!"

"Enough! I am done with yer interfering. Ye had no right to drag those people here with the promise of marriage. Do ye have any idea the heartbreak ye caused, woman?" The anger in his voice was heightened by his low growling tone.

She raised her chin, her face growing red. "'Tis not sorry I did."

Closing his eyes, he shook his head, and then fixed her with a piercing look. "'Tis too bad ye said that."

She shrugged—and that was the final straw.

Rage shot through him at her careless dismissal of what she'd done. "As yer laird, I'm ordering ye to move yer belongings to the tower. Ye will live out yer years in those rooms, taking yer meals there."

"Nay! Ye canna do that. My daughters are here."

"I will see to my sisters. 'Tis not sure I am that yer influence on them is a good one, anyway. Yer a hateful woman, and 'tis a distressing day when I need to say that to my own mum." Before he could change his mind, he pushed himself out of the chair and left the room.

In less than an hour he was clean, shaven, dressed, and ready to leave again. The food and bath had helped clear his head from the previous evening. Going to the small silver and black box on his dresser, he removed enough coins for the trip. In the corner of the box sat the ruby and diamond ring Sybil had placed on her pillow right before she'd left. Retrieving it, he rubbed the stone on his sleeve. Then fisting it, he closed his eyes and remembered the pain on her face when she'd walked in on his argument with his mum.

Whatever it took, he would gain her forgiveness and make her believe he loved her and would do whatever was necessary to make her his.

I'm coming for ye, lass.

Chapter Eighteen

The fading sun cast a soft golden glow over Sybil and Sarah as they walked arm in arm around the end of the summer roses in the east garden. "I believe I may survive, Sarah."

Sarah hugged her twin closer. "You are a strong woman, Sybil. Of course you will survive."

"There were times I truly doubted it. I finally realized how Marion felt the two years she was mourning Tristan." Sybil shook her head. "Except in my case, he isn't dead."

"Neither was Tristan."

"True." Sybil smiled. "In some crazy way it would be better. But married to someone else?"

It had taken her a couple of weeks, but she had finally confided in Sarah what had taken place in Scotland. Even the part about her and Liam making love. Instead of being shocked, her sister prodded her for information until Sybil brought a halt to the conversation. Some things were not to be shared, even with one's twin.

Sarah had sympathized with her when she had replayed

the argument with Liam. How his words proved he still held animosity and disdain for the English. She told Sarah that had they gone forward with the wedding, every time they had a disagreement, the issue of English against Scottish would most likely arise.

However, Sybil was surprised to hear her twin almost try to excuse Liam's words. She gently pointed out that after all she'd told her of Lady MacBride, it seemed the woman could certainly goad someone into saying things they truly didn't mean.

But it didn't help to dwell on that thought—it was too painful to think she'd acted in haste.

"Auntie!" Their nephew, eighteen month old Robert, Marquess of Stafford, toddled on the path toward them, followed by his mother, Penelope. Their sister-in-law pushed a pram with five month old Lady Esther Lacey.

Sybil bent and the boy ran to her. Scooping him up, she swung him around and gave him a loud smacking kiss on his cheek. "I still cannot get over how big you grew while I was gone. Surely it must have been a whole year."

"No."

Penelope laughed. "That seems to be his favorite word. That and *papa*."

Sybil rubbed her nose on Robert's belly. "Are you giving your mama a hard time, my lord?"

"No." He started to wiggle. "Down."

Once on his feet, he proceeded to squat and watch a bug wander the path. He pointed to the insect. "Bug."

"Yes, sweetheart that is a bug." Penelope was now holding Esther, making motherly clucking sounds.

At the warm and loving the scene before her, Sybil

placed her hand on her belly, the gnawing anxiety she'd felt since her return washing over her. Dear Lord, what would she do if what she suspected were true? That was another dilemma she'd shared with Sarah.

"Penelope, where is Junie?" The nanny was another in a string of nurses the Duke and his wife had employed since Robert's birth. Although she would not admit it, it was generally known in the family that Penelope wished no one but herself to deal with her children. Hence the parade of girls that she'd not found suitable for one reason or another. They'd always left the duke's employ with a generous severance and a glowing recommendation.

American-born and raised by an unconventional father who'd taught his daughter botany, Penelope was loved by the entire family. And since the dowager duchess had also broken with tradition in the raising of her children, no one thought much of Penelope's strange behavior.

"Junie had a headache, so I told her to lie down."

Sarah grinned. "Did you also bring her a cool cloth with lavender?"

"Yes, that works so well for me." Penelope reached down and stopped Robert right before the boy put the bug in his mouth.

"Penelope, you do understand the concept of servants doing for their employers, not the other way around?" Sarah was laughing now.

"Oh dear, I think this little one needs a nappy change." Penelope returned Esther to the pram and reached out for Robert's hand. "Come along, dear."

"No."

"It is time for tea."

"No." The little boy pointed to the dirt where Penelope had tossed the insect. "Bug."

"You cannot have the bug, darling. Now come along with Mama so we can have our tea."

"No."

"Go ahead and take care of the baby, Penelope. Sarah and I will get Robert into the house for tea."

The boy looked up at his aunts. "No."

With a great deal of coaxing they got Robert as far as the side door of the manor when a scuffling noise drew their attention to the entrance hall. A carriage stood in front of the manor, the door of the vehicle open, but no one inside.

With Sarah and Sybil each holding one of Robert's hands they climbed the few steps to the back door and down the corridor toward the front entrance.

"I'll not be leaving here until I see Sybil. Now either call the lass, or you'll be seeing me searching every room in the place."

Drake stood blocking the door as Sybil and Sarah hurried forward.

"Sybil!" A man's voice shouted.

Sybil's eyes widened. "Liam?"

Drake turned just enough at Sybil's words to allow Liam to shove his way in. Sybil dropped Robert's hand and covered her mouth with her fingers. "What are you doing here?"

"I've come to get ye, lass."

Drake stepped up to the couple. "I think we should move this conversation to the library."

In a daze, Sybil allowed Liam to lead her into the library behind Drake. Their mother, drawn to the racket at the front door, along with Sarah, trooped behind to join them. Once the women were all settled into chairs, Drake leaned against his desk and crossed his arms, facing Liam who stood with his feet spread apart, looking very much like a Scottish warrior.

Sybil was speechless for perhaps the first time in her life. Even though she'd been overwhelmed with anger when she'd left him, her heart now pounded in an all too familiar and exciting way. She'd forgotten how very powerful and determined Laird Liam MacBride could look. His chin stuck out and his eyes snapped as if ready to take on not just her brother, the Duke, but all of England.

What had been his purpose in coming here? The only thought in her head was how happy she was to see him. She was hard pressed to remain mad at him. She only wanted to throw herself into his arms and weep for joy.

"Perhaps you better explain to all of us exactly what went on in Scotland. My sister returned home quite a bit different than when she left to go to Lady Margaret's wedding. I had a letter from you many weeks ago telling me you were taking responsibility for my sister, she would be visiting your castle where she would be well chaperoned, and you would personally see her home safely. Does that sound familiar?"

"Yes, Yer Grace."

"Yet my sister returns with only her maid, your driver, and an outrider. She is melancholy, will not tell me what went on in Scotland, and now you appear at my front door demanding to see her as though you have some rights where she is concerned."

"Aye, ye have the right of it, mon. Perhaps I could have some time to speak with Sybil alone." Liam glanced at all the curious eyes watching the scene.

"I don't believe I trust you to be alone with my sister. I still don't know what went on in Scotland and nothing you've said so far has changed my opinion."

Liam ran stiff fingers through his hair. "I asked the lass to marry me."

"Then why did she return home? Sybil," he turned toward his sister, "did you refuse the man?"

"Yes."

Drake stepped forward. "Then you will please remove yourself from the premises."

"Wait!" Sybil jumped up. "I did refuse him at first, but then I changed my mind and we became betrothed."

"And?"

"We had some differences."

"What differences?"

"He insulted my English heritage."

Drake narrowed his eyes at Liam, then pulled back his arm and slammed his fist into Liam's chin. He went down, but was back up in a flash.

"You maligned my sister?" Her brother rubbed his knuckles.

"Nay. My mum pushed me into an argument, and Sybil overheard something I said in anger." He turned to Sybil. "I dinna mean it, lass. You have to believe me."

"Since my sister is back here in England, it appears whatever you said, my sister did believe, so I repeat, please remove yourself from the premises."

Liam turned to her. "Lass, please. I need to speak with ye alone."

Sybil stood and immediately swayed. Liam, Drake, and Sarah all reached out for her. The lightheadedness had been increasing. Which is precisely what she had been afraid of.

She was breeding.

Liam reached her first and wrapped his arm around her, tucking her into his side. "What is the matter, lass? Are ye ill?"

Sybil shook her head. The dizziness had left, but her stomach gave her reason to believe it would soon relieve itself of her luncheon. "No, I'm fine."

Drake glared at Liam. "I suggest you remove your arm from my sister and take yourself back to Scotland."

"Nay. I'll not be leaving without Sybil."

"Stop! Everyone is talking about me as if I weren't present." Her mind was reeling. Liam was here, he apparently hadn't married the woman his mother had sent for, and she was most likely pregnant. On top of that, he'd driven her away by blurting out that his children would never be English and would only know their Scottish heritage. They'd parted on not too friendly terms. To say she was confused would be an understatement.

She took in a deep breath. "Yes, we must talk, but first I need to make a quick trip." She slapped her hand on her mouth, turned, and then raced from the room, Sarah and her mother right behind her.

"Lass, I think ye are carrying my bairn."

Sybil dashed up the stairs to the sound of flesh hitting flesh and the thud of a body hitting the floor.

• • •

Liam breathed a sigh of relief as Drake reached across the desk and shook his hand. "Welcome to the family."

They'd been cosseted in the library, just the two of them, for over an hour. Liam worked his jaw that had taken two blows from his future brother-in-law. For a cushy duke, the man had a wallop. Not that he blamed Drake. Had a man taken advantage of Catriona or Alanna, he would have done the same. And more.

Once the women left the room the two men had faced each other like two snarling animals. Liam was determined to convince the Duke of Manchester that he would be a wonderful husband for his sister. The duke was obviously very protective of his women, and Liam liked that.

All the agreements had been reached and signed. He didn't care what Sybil's dowry was, he only wanted her. He was especially anxious to speak with her now that he suspected she was in a family way. Sobering at the thought of how difficult life would have been for the lass had he not decided to put aside his pride and come after her, he wanted to assure her that he was thrilled at the prospect of being a father. Also, given their last conversation, he had yet to convince her that he would not allow any child of theirs to ignore their English side. He still had a lot of groveling to do.

"I imagine you and Sybil have a few things to straighten out. I'll see if she's feeling up to it, and send her in." Apparently, once again reminded of what condition Liam had sent his sister home in, Drake frowned and hesitated before striding to the door. "I expect you to keep your hands to yourself until the marriage takes place."

"Aye." Not that it mattered, since the damage had already been done, but he didn't think it would be smart to mention that little fact to the duke.

Liam paced the area in front of the fireplace for so long he was amazed to see the rug had not been worn through. He whipped his head around as the door to the library opened.

Sybil stood there, still a bit pale.

She walked slowly into the room. The happiness he'd been hoping to see in her eyes was missing. She looked guarded, on edge, not at all how he'd hoped their reunion to be. Despite him and her brother agreeing on terms, it appeared he still had a problem where the lass was concerned.

He drew on all the charm he'd used over the years with the fairer sex. "Darlin', 'tis sorry I am. For everything. For my mum, for what I said about our bairns, and for blurting out about yer condition before yer family."

She crossed her arms and tapped her foot. "Why are you here, Liam?"

He reached his hand out. "Come here, lass, and sit."

She took the chair near the fireplace. With a grunt, he scooped her up and settled her on his lap. Her body stiff, she held herself back. "Please answer my question."

"I am here to bring you back to Bedlay with me. Where you belong. As my wife, and if I'm not mistaken, as the mother of my bairn."

"Why?"

"Because I love you."

"Love requires trust and acceptance. You don't accept the English part of me. Any children we would have," she paused and covered her belly, "would be half English."

"Aye, and proud of them I will be."

She gave a very unladylike snort.

After all this, was he going to lose her? Just because he had blurted out something stupid in the middle of an argument?

Nay. He would fight for what he wanted. He would not give up now, even if he had to camp outside her door for the next year. "I love you, lass. With my whole heart." He grasped her chin and made her face him. "Can you honestly say you don't love me?"

"No," she whispered. "I can't say that. But will that be enough?"

"If you turn me away, you are basing that decision on a dislike of the English I held all the years before I met you that had been drummed into me since birth." He kissed the tips of her fingers. "I can learn, darlin'. You can help me."

"The first time we have a disagreement, you'll be spouting off about the English." She moved off his lap and faced him. "And our children? Will they face your disdain if they show anything other than Scottish ways?"

"Nay." He reached out to pull her to him, but she danced away.

He stiffened his shoulders and regarded her. "All right, Sybil. I will tell ye what we will do."

"What?" She viewed him through narrowed eyes.

"Come sit here next to me." He reached out again. "Please?"

She edged over and rested her bottom on the end of the chair.

He took a deep breath. "I will send word to my cousin Damian that he is now The MacBride. I will relinquish my title and clan to stay here in England with you. I have enough of my own funds that we can purchase an estate anywhere you desire and raise our bairns to be English."

• • •

Sybil sucked in a breath, her eyes wide, Surely her ears had deceived her? It was not possible that she'd heard correctly.

"You don't mean that." Liam would leave his clan? Leave Scotland?

"I do." He took her hand in his. "I mean it with every beat of my heart. If I canna have ye, nothing else matters. 'Twould be difficult, to be sure, but for ye I would do it." He kissed her fingers. "And I would never regret it."

"Oh, Liam."

Before she could say another word, he cupped the back of her head and brought her mouth to his. Gently, he teased her lips, rubbing his against hers until she smiled. Encouraged, he drew her closer and deepened the kiss with all the pent up love and desire in his heart.

"Ach, lass. Just say the word, and we will be married as soon as yer brother can arrange it. I'll begin a search for a home here." He cupped her cheeks and kissed her mouth, jaw, nose, eyes, and chin.

Her eyes burning with tears, she pulled back to stare into his face. "I think I may be carrying your bairn."

He grinned at her use of that word. "Aye, so it seems, with ye racing out of the room before, lookin' as green as the hills of Scotland." He crushed her to him. "Thank God I'll be able to take care of ye and the bairn." Taking her hand, he said, "I promise this is the last time I'll ask this question, darlin'. Will ye marry me?"

One lone tear tracked down her cheek. "Yes, my laird, I will marry you."

"I feel as though we've done this before," he said as he slipped the heavy ring on her finger.

"I believe you are right." Sybil ran her fingertip over the ring and smiled. "This time I will never give it back."

"Nay. And I'll never take it back." He grinned, relief

spreading through him. "We need to plan a wedding again and begin our search for a home."

"I'm afraid that, given my condition, Drake will want the wedding as soon as possible. However…"

"What?"

"I'll not allow you to give up your clan." She raised her hand as he began to speak. "By the mere fact that you were willing to do it convinces me you will try very hard to make sure our children know and appreciate both their Scottish and English heritages."

He tugged her to him and settled her once again on his lap. "I really would stay in England with ye."

"I know." She brushed back the hair from his forehead. "And as much as I love you for that, I would not be happy if you did. After all, our son would be the next Laird MacBride one day. How can I deprive him of that?"

The door flew open and Drake barreled into the room. "I believe you've had enough time to get things settled." He narrowed his eyes. "Get off his lap. You can have time alone together once the wedding is over."

Liam and Sybil grinned at each other as the dowager duchess, Sarah, and two other women crowded into the room.

Sybil stood and drew the women over. "Liam, may I present my sister, Mary, and sister-in-law Penelope." Taking Liam's arm, she said, "Allow me to introduce you to Liam, Laird of Clan MacBride. My betrothed."

He bowed before each woman, then turned to Sarah. "And since ye look so much like my Sybil, you must be her twin, Sarah."

"Oh, I am sorry," Sybil said. "With all the commotion before, I didn't realize I hadn't introduced you to my mother and Sarah."

"It is a pleasure to meet you, Liam." The dowager duchess linked her arm in Sybil's "My dear, due to the circumstances, we have to put this together rather quickly, I'm afraid."

Sybil blushed slightly, embarrassed her mother knew the reason for the hurried nuptials.

• • •

Sybil settled back in the carriage and gave a deep sigh. They were finally married. Her mother had managed to put together a lovely wedding in only two weeks. Drake had allowed Liam to stay in the manor, but walked him to his bedchamber each night, and then roused him at dawn each morning for a "ride."

Since she'd never known Drake to be fond of early morning forays, she could only assume he was making sure Liam stayed in his own room each night. As much as she would have liked to wake up with Liam's warm arms around her, the wedding preparations kept her busy enough to not dwell on it.

Liam had fit in with her family as if he'd known them for years. Her brother and her betrothed had spent time not only riding at the break of dawn, but also behind closed doors, discussing their respective estates. Her sisters had been charmed by the Scottish burr, and her young nephew had climbed onto Liam's lap every evening for a story.

The whirlwind wedding took place in the village chapel with her brother-in-law, Rector Joseph Fox, officiating. Her mother and sisters had wiped tears from their eyes as she said her vows while Penelope had chased Robert down the aisle as he headed for the new friend who'd told him wonderful Scottish tales at night.

The next morning Sybil had awoken feeling loved and cared for after a wedding night that hadn't allowed for very much sleep. Despite the desire running rampant through them as they'd fumbled with buttons and ties to remove each other's clothes, Liam hadn't rushed, loving every part of her body. He had also spent a good deal of time kissing and talking to her belly where the babe rested.

She winced at the various aches and pains in unfamiliar places, evidencing their hours of exploring each other's bodies with no concern about being interrupted. It had truly been a night she would remember all her life.

Leaning out the carriage window, she waved a final good-bye to her family. They all stood outside, her mother patting her eyes with a handkerchief and Sarah looking lost. As the carriage jerked, then eased as the horses moved into a smooth cadence, Sybil studied the stately home where she had grown up.

She smiled at the large oak tree where her sister, Abigail, quite young at the time, had been tied up. Drake and Abigail's now-husband, Joseph, had done the deed because she wouldn't stop following them about.

As the carriage began its descent down the pebbled path, they passed the pond where they'd all learned to swim. She could almost see a young Marion and her husband, Tristan, when he had tried to teach her to float on her back without panicking. He'd been so patient with her. A lot more patient than Drake and Joseph had been with Abigail.

They passed the hill where her mother had taken them sledding so often. They'd engaged in snowball fights and built snowmen with coal for the eyes and large carrots for their noses. There was even the time they'd all been sent to bed without their dinner because they'd stolen Papa's best hat for a snowman and it had been accidentally trampled by a horse.

She sighed and leaned back against the soft leather seat. When she'd left for Margaret's wedding, it had been with the idea of returning in several weeks. Now she knew any return here would be as a guest.

Liam took her hand in his. "I told yer brother we would welcome his visit anytime he wants to travel our way."

"Thank you." She used the tip of her handkerchief to catch the tear that slid from her eye. "I will miss my sister, Sarah, dreadfully. Except for Margaret's wedding, we have never been apart."

"Ach, lass. When it grows near yer time, invite yer sister to come stay with us."

"Yes. I think that is a splendid idea." Her bright smile brought a grin to her husband's face as well.

"'Tis been quite a couple of weeks for ye, lass. And with yer condition and all, I think a short nap will ease ye, and help the time pass." With a quick movement, he scooped her up from the seat and settled her on his lap. "Sleep now."

Annoyed at being ordered to nap like a child, she held her tongue when she realized how very tired she was. After a healthy yawn, she cuddled close to the warmth and security of Liam's chest. Before falling into a sound sleep, her last thought was of meeting Lady MacBride when they arrived at Bedlay Castle.

The only thorn among all the roses in her life. But, unfortunately, a very large barb.

Chapter Nineteen

"Liam, we must speak of your mother." Sybil adjusted her skirts as they neared the inn that was their first stop along the way to Bedlay Castle. She'd enjoyed a nice long nap, and now her stomach reminded her that she was eating for two people.

"'Twill not be a problem. Dinna fash yerself, lass."

"You've said that every time I've asked. In a few days we will be back at Bedlay. I don't wish to say unkind things about your mother, but I don't see her being happy about our marriage."

"I've banished her."

Sybil gasped. "What?"

"I had her move into the tower section of the castle. She has all the comforts of the main castle, but cannot cause mischief."

"Oh, no. I don't like that. I feel terrible that she was banished."

"After what she did? Aye lass, ye are much too soft."

"But she is your mother. Even though what she did was hurtful, she loves you, and only wanted what she thought was best."

His lips tightened and he waved his hand. "'Tis done. There is no reason to speak on it further."

Sybil thought of her own mother and how adored she was by all her family. She placed her hand on her grumbling stomach. One day Lady MacBride would be a grandmother. With her dislike of all things English, would she dismiss the child? Despite what the woman had done, it would be difficult for her and Liam to have true happiness with the babe's only nearby grandmother banished.

• • •

Sybil experienced a sense of familiarity as their carriage crested the hill leading to Bedlay Castle, and two young girls raced from the front door. Catriona and Alanna abandoned all dignity as they lifted their skirts and dashed toward them.

"You came back!" Catriona threw herself into Sybil's arms as soon as she stepped out of the carriage.

"Aye, she did come back. As my wife," Liam said as he received a hug from Alanna.

"You got married!" Alanna gripped Sybil's hand and examined the gold and diamond wedding band Liam had placed on her finger during the ceremony only five days ago.

"We are truly sisters now," Alanna said.

"Yes, we are, and I am so happy to have you both as such. You will help me deal with not having my sisters about."

Both girls wrapped their arms around Sybil's waist as they moved toward the front door. "What about our clan,

Liam? I thought as laird you had to be married in front of the clan?" Catriona asked.

"Aye. There will be a wedding here as soon as the three of you can arrange it."

They entered the drawing room and Alanna turned to Liam. "What about Mum?"

"I'm sure the three of ye can do what needs to be done. I will ride for the priest in the morning. Sybil, ye can talk with Mrs. MacDougal and get everything seen to."

Catriona and Alanna glanced at each other, their wide smiles diminishing somewhat. Sybil already loved her new sisters, and if she could make things right for them then she had to try.

• • •

It was about an hour after dinner and Liam was busy in the library with matters that needed to be taken care of since his absence. Catriona and Alanna had settled at the chessboard, as usual.

"I am feeling a bit spent from our journey. If you will excuse me, I will retire early."

"Good night, Sybil," the girls echoed.

"I will join ye in a bit." Liam glanced up as he reached for another ledger.

Instead of heading upstairs, Sybil took a light woolen wrap from the entrance hall and left the castle. A short, somewhat muddy, walk led her to the tower area. She glanced up to see a light flickering at the very top of the structure. Lady MacBride had not yet retired. Taking a deep breath, and hoping she would not make things worse, she opened the latch on the large wooden door, held her candle up, and stepped into the area.

It was damp and dismal. Despite it being late summer, there was a definite chill in the air. She shivered and ran her hand up and down her arm. As she moved farther in, a winding staircase came into view on her right side. She held the candle high to observe the room, but the staircase was the only way to the top.

The climb was not difficult, but not something she would want to do several times a day. Since Liam would not speak of his mother's banishment, she had no way of knowing how the woman was being fed. It would be daunting for Mrs. MacDougal to have to deliver meals here three times a day. Although, most likely one of the younger kitchen girls would be sent. But it still seemed a sad and lonely existence for Lady MacBride.

At the very top of the stairs, three doors appeared. The one straight ahead and to her left would not be in a position for her to see the light flickering. Placing her hand on her stomach, she knocked softly on the door to her right.

"Come."

Sybil opened the door. Lady MacBride sat on a comfortable looking chair, her needle poised over a large frame of some type of needlework. Her expression went from a slight smile to a sneer. "So, ye came back?"

"Yes." Although she hadn't been invited to sit, Sybil walked to the chair directly across from her mother-in-law and rested on the very edge. Placing the candle in a holder on a small table, she rested her hands in her lap.

"I see the ring on yer finger, so I guess the laird married ye, after all."

"Yes." If she hadn't been studying Lady MacBride so closely she might have missed the slight softening of her face.

Then the woman drew herself up, and said, "I suppose ye've come to prance about and let me ken ye won."

Sybil shook her head. "No, my lady. Not at all."

Lady MacBride shrugged. "Dinna fash yerself, lass. Ye won, so ye can just be on yer way."

Sybil rose and crossed the small space between them. Dropping to her knees, she took the woman's hands in hers, being careful to avoid the needle, lest her mother-in-law decide to stab her. "We have a great deal in common, you know."

"Ach. What would I have in common with a Sassenach?"

Sybil took the needle from her hand and placed it on the frame. "We both love the same man."

"Ach, you dinna love Liam. Ye want only what he can give ye."

"You are so wrong, my lady. I love Liam very much." She released Lady MacBride's hands and sat back on her heels. "In my family, no one marries for any reason other than love. It is what you might call a tradition. There have been one or two that didn't start out that way, but both of my sisters and my brother enjoy very happy marriages."

She tilted her head. "I waited through four London Seasons to find the right man. Someone whom I could love with my whole heart and who would love me the same. I never would have guessed that the reason I hadn't found him in a London ballroom was because all that time he was in a Scottish castle."

Lady MacBride gave her a slight smile. "Ye have a way with words, lass. I will give ye that."

Heartened by the woman's response, she continued, "Then hear my words and believe them. I don't think my husband will be truly happy if his mother is relegated to the tower."

Lady MacBride shook her head. "Nay, lass. The laird has turned against me. Ye see before ye a stubborn, foolish woman."

"Then perhaps your stubborn, foolish son can see the error of his ways."

Shaking her head, but not quite so determinedly, she said, "Nay, he had the right of it. 'Twas a mean thing I did to him." She glanced at Sybil. "And to ye, too."

"But it has all turned out well."

When the woman didn't answer, Sybil said, "We will be having a full Scottish wedding in a few days. I would be very happy if you are there."

"Why would ye want me there, lass? I caused ye nothing but trouble and heartache."

Sybil rose and adjusted her skirts. "For two reasons, my lady. One, I love your son too much to cause him any distress on his wedding day. I don't think he would enjoy it to the fullest unless you are there with us." Picking up her candle, she headed to the door. She turned as she reached for the latch. "And I'll be lettin' ye ken a secret. Since there is a wee bairn on the way, 'tis important to make peace with yer son. Aye?"

She quietly closed the door and held firmly onto the stone wall as she descended the stairs to return to the castle. The sound of soft laughter floated in the air from behind the bedchamber door.

• • •

Even though it was her second wedding day, for some reason Sybil felt more nervous than the first time around. Maybe it was the idea of facing Liam's entire clan as his bride, or worry that his mother would or would not appear.

With the help of Mrs. MacDougal, the three girls were able to get everything finished and ready on time. The priest had arrived early yesterday, and the guests had gathered in the chapel a short distance from the castle. Lady Margaret and Duncan had hurried in a bit ago, apologizing for their tardiness, but it seemed the new bride was breeding and had a bit of trouble holding onto her breakfast.

Taking one last look in the mirror, Sybil laid her hand on her middle and took a deep breath.

"We must go, Sybil. 'Tis growing late." Alanna's anxious voice drew her from her musing.

"I am ready."

Because of the muddy roads, Sybil, Catriona, and Alanna all rode in the carriage to the chapel. The small church was built of smooth stone and had stood on the same spot for more than two hundred years. All the MacBride lairds had married there, and all the MacBride clan members had been buried there.

Sybil clutched the skirts of her pale blue gown as she took the few steps from the carriage to the chapel door. She entered and was immediately taken with the sight of Liam once again dressed in full clan attire. He turned as she stepped into the chapel and extended his hand. Laird Liam MacBride was impressive at any time, but in his formal Highlander dress he was indeed a sight to behold.

She stepped next to him, and they faced the priest.

"Wait just a minute, there, Father." Lady MacBride

walked the short distance from the door to the front pew. "I want to be sure to see my laird marry his lady."

Sybil nearly laughed at the shocked look on Liam's face. She tugged his arm so he leaned down. "I invited her."

He grinned from ear to ear. "Ye never cease to amaze me, lass."

They turned to face the priest to once more take their vows. This time in front of the entire Clan MacBride.

Epilogue

"Ach, lass, how many times do I need to tell ye to stop doin' so much and rest yerself?" Lady MacBride bustled into the drawing room, catching Sybil attempting to put a book back on a shelf above her head.

"I am fine. Truly." She moved her bulky body to the settee and eased down. "Though I feel as if I swallowed an entire watermelon."

"Never ye mind. Ye have to take better care of that bairn yer carrying. Ach, what can I do with ye?" She fisted her hands on her hips. "I'm going to have yer laird tie ye to the bed."

"I don't believe that is necessary." Sybil shifted, uncomfortable no matter how she adjusted herself.

"Mayhap it is." Liam strode into the room and frowned at his wife. "Yer lookin' mighty tired, darlin'." He scooped Sybil up and settled her in his arms.

"Liam, put me down." Sybil laughed. "You will hurt your back carrying me." Despite her protests, she was grateful to have his strong arms around her. She was indeed very tired, and the ache in her back had only grown worse as the day went on.

"Ach, the day I cannot carry a wee thing like ye 'tis the day I'll take to my bed for the last time."

"Don't be silly. I must weigh as much as an elephant."

"Nay. Hardly more than my broadsword."

They trudged up the stairs and down the corridor to their bedchamber, where he gently deposited her on the counterpane. "Now rest, lass."

Sybil reached out and touched his arm, urging him to sit alongside her on the bed. "Has there been word from Sarah today?"

Liam sighed. "Nay. I canna understand what is taking the lass so long."

"I'm frightened. She left London two weeks ago." Sybil had written to her twin when she'd passed the sixth month of her pregnancy. At Liam's suggestion, she had asked her to make the trip to the Highlands to be with her when the babe arrived. In a note delivered two weeks ago, Sarah stated she would be leaving the next day. Unless something dreadful had happened to her, she should have arrived days ago.

"Dinna fash yerself, lass. She has her maid with her, a driver, and a footman. If something happened along the road it might not have been possible for her to send a note. I'm sure all is well." He drew the bed curtains, blocking out the sun. "Now rest yerself."

"Don't leave." Sybil stopped his movement with her hand. "Can you rub my back? It's been bothering me all day."

"Sure, darlin'. Turn over and I'll give ye a good rub."

Sybil rolled her bulk to the side just as a sharp pain shot

from her back to around her front. "Oh." She doubled up, clasping her stomach and breaking into a sweat.

"What?" Liam jumped up. "Is it the bairn?"

"I think so." She took a deep breath. "Oh, that hurt."

"'Tis time for Mum." He raced from the room, practically knocking Bessie over as she entered.

"What is it, my lady? Is the babe coming?"

"I think so, Bessie. Here, help me out of these clothes and into a nightgown."

With fumbling fingers the young maid got her changed and settled back into bed just as a gush of water released, wetting her and the bed.

"Oh, Bessie, I'm so sorry."

"Ach, lass, 'tis time." Lady MacBride hustled into the room with linens and a pile of soft cloths. "Bessie, get her changed."

"Where is Liam?" Sybil asked and then panted as another pain gripped her.

"I sent him for the midwife. He canna be here, anyway." She wiped Sybil's forehead with a cool cloth. "Just relax, lass. 'Twill be a while until the bairn arrives."

• • •

Liam counted the steps once again. Thirty-four in one direction, twenty-seven in another. He'd done it so many times he could do it with his eyes closed. He stopped and cocked his ear. Sybil had been wailing for some time now, each cry a knife to his heart. 'Twas the last bairn he'd put in her. He couldn't live through this again.

He wiped the sweat from his forehead, turned on his heel, and counted again. The door to the library flew open, almost hitting him square in the head. Catriona stood there, her mouth agape.

"What?"

"The bairn," she whispered.

Before she could speak further, his head snapped up at the wail of a different sort. A strange cry, somewhat like the shriek of a cat. He grabbed Catriona by her shoulders. "The bairn?"

"Aye."

He rushed past her, almost knocking the girl over, and took the stairs two at a time. Racing down the corridor, he barely avoided crashing into Bessie as she left the room.

"My laird, a wonderful day. A wonderful day, indeed."

Liam nodded and continued on. He entered the bedchamber. His mum held a tiny bundle, gazing down with amazement. She looked up at him, tears in her eyes. "A lass."

A lass!

He broke into a grin and turned to the bed where Sybil lay, her eyes bright. She had been cleaned up and her hair was braided. In her arms lay a tiny bundle. He moved toward her, his eyebrows raised.

"A son," she whispered.

He licked his dry lips. "Two?"

"Aye," she said. "Two."

Liam sat alongside her, running his knuckles down her soft cheek. He used his finger to edge back the small blanket and looked down at the most beautiful sight he'd ever seen. A tiny head with ginger colored hair, his eyes closed in peaceful slumber.

Mum walked over and put his daughter in his arms. She kissed Sybil and Liam both on the head and left the room.

"*Tha gaol agam ort*," Liam whispered to his darling English wife.

"*Tha gaol agam ort-fhèin*," she answered her strong Scottish warrior.

They spent the next ten minutes counting fingers and toes on their English-Scottish bairns.

Author's Note

There wasn't a lot of information available on post-Culloden and the Clearances in Scotland, so I used my regency knowledge to fill in what I couldn't get actual facts for. For those of you familiar with Scottish history, if there are mistakes, they are mine, alone.

If I left you wondering what happened to Sybil's twin, Sarah, watch for the release of the sixth Marriage Mart Mayhem novel, *The Highlander's Accidental Marriage* coming in late 2015.

Acknowledgments

The Highlander's Choice is the fifth book my fabulous editor, Erin McCormack Molta and I have worked on together. Her suggestions are always spot on, and make the story so much better. And she does a wonderful job of cleaning up my grammar and pointing out *pluperfect active verbs*.

About the Author

USA Today bestselling author of *The Elusive Wife*, Callie Hutton writes both Western Historical and Regency romance, with "historic elements and sensory details" (*The Romance Reviews*). She also pens an occasional contemporary or two. Callie lives in Oklahoma with several rescue dogs, two adult children, and daughter-in-law (thankfully all not in the same house), and her top cheerleader husband of thirty-eight years. She also recently welcomed twin grandsons to her ever expanding family. Callie loves to hear from readers, and would welcome you as a "friend" on Facebook. You can contact her through her website: www.calliehutton.com, or write her directly at calliehutton11@gmail.com

Made in the USA
Middletown, DE
15 July 2022

69400917R00139